Book I: The Salacir Chronicles

What Lies Beyond

Hannah Jeffers-Huser

Book I: The Salacir Chronicles

What Lies Beyond

Hannah Jeffers-Huser

A MEADOWLARK BOOK

Meadowlark (an imprint of Chasing Tigers Press)
meadowlark-books.com
PO Box 333
Emporia, KS 66801

Cover photography-Evie Simmons;
model-Maddie Simmons; digital art-Kaman Simmons

Author Photo by Jennifer Cox

ISBN: 978-0-9966801-7-2

Library of Congress Control Number: 2017915463

for my friends and family

Prologue

Screams could be heard echoing throughout King Roland's palace. The king paced back and forth outside of the room where the cries were coming from. His advisor, an aged man named Eyra, placed a comforting hand on his king's shoulder.

"Everything will be all right, Your Majesty. Queen Abry and Aria's heir will both be healthy." Eyra spoke calmly, his deep voice doing very little to provide comfort to the king. This was, after all, his first child, and most likely his last. He and the queen tried for many years before she finally conceived and he feared she would not be able to conceive again.

One last pain filled scream ripped through the palace air before the shrill sound of a baby's cry could be heard. It seemed like an eternity passed before a servant stepped from the room and curtsied to the king.

"King Roland," she said. "You may enter now. The queen and child are both healthy." The servant quickly moved out of the way to allow the king entrance. Once inside, he saw his wife sitting in bed holding a small bundle in her arms. The baby was still crying, but he paid no attention to the noise. Queen Abry's tired amber eyes beamed at her husband, her curly, black hair sticking to her sweaty, mocha colored skin.

"Would you like to meet your son, Love?" she asked. She could barely contain her excitement as she held the baby boy out to his father. King Roland carefully took him into his own arms, noticing the boy had his dark brown hair. Eyra stood on the other side of the woman's bedside. His eyes widened when he noticed a small, diamond-shaped birthmark on the baby's forehead.

"Your Majesties, your child is a special one," Eyra spoke as he leaned toward the baby. Queen Abry glanced at the advisor and then her husband. She had no doubts about her child being special. This boy would one day rule Aria.

The king and queen looked to the advisor for an explanation, waiting for the old man to continue.

"This child has the mark of the diamond," Eyra began. "Years ago, I had a vision about this mark, but I was never shown who the mark would belong to. Your son is destined to change and save our world from destruction as a Peace Bringer."

Queen Abry stared at her son in astonishment. Salacir had not needed a Peace Bringer for over a century. The countries were not at war. The only obstruction to that peace would have to come from the ruthless savages that were scattered about the lands.

"He and one other baby born this very night will bring two worlds together to destroy the evil forces that will come to surround Aria and the rest of Salacir."

King Roland looked down at the child in his arms. "Prince Adair of Aria, you will one day bring greatness and honor to our country."

The baby opened his eyes to reveal the deep blue color resembling his father's. King Roland had never felt more proud.

Prince Adair was not the only baby born that autumn evening. Another woman in Aria was in labor. She belonged to the Avory clan, a tribe of warriors that lived within Aria's borders, but her people were not subjects to the crown and did not follow Arian law. Her husband, the Avory leader, had left with many of the other warriors to hunt. She let out a throaty groan as her struggle came to an end. Wails filled the room as the clan's healer held up a tiny baby girl. The mother extended her arms as the other woman swaddled the child before placing the baby in her mother's arms.

"My beautiful daughter." The woman smiled as she ran a finger through the child's silky, red hair to try to silence her crying.

The midwife leaned over the mother and chuckled. "My Lady, it seems she has your family's red hair, just like her brothers."

The woman laughed and her baby's eyes opened to reveal the beautiful, emerald green that were an exact replica of her mother's.

"Mariana, how far are Roka and the others from the village?" she asked. Her baby was early. Her husband had left to hunt thinking the baby would not arrive until after he returned. She knew he had wanted to be here.

The midwife was about to respond when the door to the room burst open and in stepped a tall, burly man. He sported a well-trimmed beard that matched his dark, brown hair. A lanky older man followed close behind him.

"Elexia!" His deep voice rang throughout the room, startling the baby and causing her to screech.

Elexia put a pale finger to her lips. "Roka, shush. You're scaring her."

A smile danced across Roka's lips. "A girl, huh? After three sons, we finally managed to have a daughter."

Elexia smiled as she coaxed the baby to sleep with a lullaby. "She looks just like her brothers," she said with a smile.

"They all get that red hair from you." Roka teased his wife. Elexia let out a soft and melodic chuckle as she passed the child to her husband.

Roka held the baby carefully in his arms as an old man came to his side to look at the child. He stared at the tiny diamond birthmark on the child's neck.

"Teller Seyu, is something wrong?" Elexia gave the elder man a worried look.

The elder shook his head, "No, but your child has a destiny mark. She will be a Peace Bringer."

"Excuse me?" Elexia cocked her head to the side to glance at the child's mark.

Teller Seyu nodded. "Some seers call it the mark of the diamond. It means that this young girl is destined to bring two worlds together to bring peace to Salacir."

"But Salacir is already in a time of peace. The three great countries have not been at war for half a century," Elexia said. "And we only have the occasional scuffle with our enemies."

"War will rage and tear through the lands in the years to come. When that time does come, your daughter will be one of the Peace Bringers who stops it." He spoke as if this information was common knowledge.

Roka stared down into the green orbs of his precious newborn daughter.

"Then her name shall be Halona," the proud father said. He ran a large finger over the tiny mark on the baby's neck.

"Halona," Elexia said, giving her husband a wide smile. "A beautiful name with a perfect meaning."

Teller Seyu bowed to the couple before exiting the room to give them some space with their newest child. As he left the village's medical hut, he looked up into the sky.

"Dearest Moon, watch over that child," he said with a chuckle as he traversed the streets of Avory village. That baby girl would be the key to their future. He only hoped he would still be alive to see it happen.

Chapter 1

Everyone in the ballroom turned to stare as the Royal family made their entrance. The king and queen were known to throw parties whenever their son had accomplished something. Parties were a regular Arian affair, and parties hosted by the king and queen were the best of the best.

Prince Adair stood on his father's right, while his mother stood to the left. He could hardly contain his excitement, although, to anyone other than his mother, he appeared to be very composed. His hair was the only thing out of place. The shaggy, brown curls on his head never wanted to cooperate. Adair could see his mother's hand twitching; she wanted to fix his hair, but kept her hand at her side.

His father had taught the boy at a young age that composure was one of the most important things about being king. Adair, never wanting to disappoint his father, always tried his best to remain calm during public events, especially at events where he was the guest of honor.

King Roland stood tall in front of the crowd as he began his speech. "Today, my son embarks on another journey into adulthood. There will be another Royal Hunt tonight, but I will not be attending. He will be leading it on his own. This will help him learn how to lead when I am no longer around to advise him. He will be of age to take the throne soon. He must be ready to ascend when the time comes."

The crowd applauded as King Roland ended his announcement and ordered the festivities to start. Servants brought food into the ballroom, setting the trays of expensive meats, cheeses, and breads on the long tables at the far side of the room. The family took their places on their thrones as people began dancing on the floor below them.

"Son, why don't you go dance with a few of the young women here," his father suggested. "I'm sure Lady Alya would love to dance." King Roland gestured toward a pretty, young girl with curly blond hair. She was standing off to the side of the dance floor as her father spoke with other nobles. Her gaze wandered until it fell upon Adair. Her cheeks flushed as the prince met her eyes.

"Father, I have no interest in Lady Alya." Adair said, moving his eyes from the girl to glance at his father.

"Adair, you are going to have to find a wife eventually. How do you expect to have an heir if you have no woman to birth you one?" the king said, sighing.

Queen Abry placed a hand on her husband's arm. "Dear, he will find the right girl when the time comes. He is only twenty," she said. "Don't you remember how long you waited before asking me to marry you?"

King Roland let out a deep sigh, knowing his wife was right. "All right, Abry, you win, but the boy should have a little fun before the hunt." He gave his son a hard pat on the back to encourage him to get on his feet. It failed to take effect.

Adair rolled his eyes. His parents always talked about him as if he were not there. He stood, itching to get away from their senseless babbling, to do exactly as his father suggested. It was not that he wanted to dance with the obnoxious woman, but he could not stand the lovesick looks his parents were giving each other as they talked about their courtship. His father had done something strange among royals and nobles. He married Abry for love instead of monetary gain. Adair's mother had not been a noble. She came from a family of bakers.

As Prince Adair walked around the dancing bodies, he noticed his father's advisor, Eyra. Adair shivered at the strange look the old man was giving him. The old geezer was always staring as if judging him. Adair recalled the day he spoke to his father about the man's rudeness.

"Father, why do you insist on keeping that demented old man around?" sixteen-year-old Adair asked.

King Roland gave his son a hearty laugh. "Eyra is not a demented old man, Adair. You must remember that Eyra is one of my most trusted advisors. He has a vast amount of knowledge on Salacir's history. He knows the prophecies."

Adair scoffed. "The prophecies are a bunch of rubbish."

King Roland gave the boy a stern look and said, "As a Peace Bringer, you are part of a prophecy, my boy. I would not speak so unkindly of them. You are destined to be a great leader one day because of the prophecy Eyra made at your birth. You cannot escape your destiny. Sooner or later, it will catch up to you."

Adair sneered at the memory and turned his head away from the ancient man's stares. He approached Alya with a handsome smile. He resisted the urge to roll his eyes as she clumsily curtsied to him. Her face turned pink as she watched the twenty-year-old extend his hand to her.

"Hello, Lady Alya," the prince said with a bow. "Would you allow me the honor of dancing with you?"

Alya said nothing, but nodded as she took the prince's hand. Adair slowly led the girl to the dance floor. He rested on hand on her waist as he took her hand in his other. Alya's face became more flushed with each passing second.

The couple waltzed across the ballroom dance floor. Alya seemed bothered by the stares of the crowd while Adair only smirked. He was accustomed to people showing curiosity and the whispers that came with being Prince of Aria. Being part of the Royal family meant he was always being watched.

He knew this girl would never make a good queen. She was too shy and timid. That's what annoyed him the most about her. Although, he assumed no Arian woman would ever be good enough to be his queen. All the women he had ever met seemed incapable of looking past his title. Most women were so afraid of offending him that they usually kept quiet. He didn't mind the silence, but he wanted a queen who could carry a conversation without being timid. Alya was simply too shy.

"So, um, Prince Adair?" Alya whispered.

"Hmm?" He gazed down at her with an eyebrow raised.

She squeaked before replying nervously, "Are you excited for your hunt?"

He faked a warm smile before answering, "Of course. This will be the first one without Father."

Alya bobbed her head and spoke so quietly the prince had to lean in and nearly come to a standstill to hear what she was saying. "But aren't you worried about the savages? I heard that they are particularly nasty this time of year."

"Of course not. We won't be near their lands. They should be worried about me if they cross the border."

The music stopped and the dance ended. Adair put a hand over his chest and bowed to the girl while she curtsied.

"Thank you for that wonderful dance, Lady Alya."

He did not give her a chance to respond before he headed back to his parents. King Roland and Queen Abry were having an animated conversation.

"Roland, I do not think Adair going out tonight is a good idea. The savages are unpredictable." Queen Abry frantically waved her hands.

King Roland sat on his throne, calm and levelheaded, as he watched his wife. He opened his mouth to speak, but closed it as his son walked over. Queen Abry frowned, but no longer voiced her displeasure. She let out a defeated sigh before walking away to talk with another high-class woman. Adair's gaze followed his mother's form as she retreated. He believed she had nothing to worry about, but had to admit her fears were justified. The savage tribes that lived throughout Salacir were bloodthirsty barbarians. Many legends and rumors surrounded the clans. One story was that they wore the bones of fingers from their victims on cords around their necks and the borders of their territories were fenced with spikes that held scalped heads.

King Roland let out an exasperated breath as he gave his son another pat on the back. "You know how she worries."

Adair nodded and was about to respond when he noticed a friend who was finishing a dance with a young woman.

"Excuse me, Father," the prince said and bowed his head before rushing off to meet his friend. The man was a few years older, and the woman he had been dancing with stayed on his arm as the prince approached.

"Good afternoon, Your Highness," the man spoke as he bowed and his wife curtsied. His long, sandy-blond hair was loosely tied at the nape of his neck. He and Adair were the same height, but this man was much thinner than the muscular prince.

"You don't need to be so formal, Bennett," Adair laughed. He rolled his eyes before smiling at the woman. "Hello, Alicia, how have you been?"

The woman smiled. "I have been well. I'm sure Bennett told you our news?" She could barely hold in her own excitement. She had a tiny frame and was much shorter than her husband. Her light, brown hair was pulled tightly into a bun and her large brown eyes seemed to shine under the lights in the ballroom.

Adair let out a deep laugh as he gave his friend a hard pat on the back. "He did. Congratulations. You don't mind if I borrow your husband for a moment, do you?"

Alicia shook her head and allowed the two men to head off together. Once Adair had the man away from his wife, his smile faded.

"Bennett, are you positive that you still want to come? You may stay here with your wife if you wish," Adair offered.

Bennett shook his head and raised his hands. "No. This will probably be the last time I will be able to hunt. This is a big event for you, Adair, and I would not miss it for the world."

Adair could not argue with the man. He trusted Bennett more than he trusted his own father, at times. He planned on making

Bennett an advisor once he became king. If Bennett still wanted to come, he would not force the man to stay.

"I saw you dancing with Lady Alya." Bennett changed the subject with a sly smirk playing on his lips.

Adair shrugged off his friend's comment and did not offer a reply. Bennett sighed. He respected Prince Adair, and he knew the young man would eventually need to marry. It was Adair's duty to provide an heir for Aria since he was an only child. Bennett let out another sigh as he shook his head. "My friend, a good king does not whine and moan. A good king does as he should for the good of his people."

Adair groaned. "Not you too. I have already been lectured by my parents. I don't need my closest friend lecturing me as well."

Bennett placed a boney hand on Adair's shoulder. "You are the only way your family's bloodline can continue. You know that as well as anyone."

It was Adair's turn to sigh. Bennett was his loyal friend, and Adair usually took his advice, but the prince loved adventure. The thought of settling down now made him sick to his stomach.

The party was coming to an end. Adair bid his friend farewell, for the time being, as he joined his parents at their thrones. King Roland gave another quick speech before the guests began to dissipate.

Adair watched as Alicia and Bennett shared a passionate kiss before she was escorted to a carriage waiting outside. Once his wife was gone, Bennett approached the Royal family. He gave the king and queen a bow.

"Please be safe, Adair." Queen Abry kissed her son's forehead. Adair glanced at Bennett and noticed the man's smirk.

"I will be fine, Mother." Adair took her hand in his and gave it a reassuring squeeze before he kissed her cheek.

"He will be fine, Love. Remember, he is destined for greatness. He can't fulfill the prophecy if he is dead," King Roland joked as he gave his son a hard pat on the back. His wife sent him a harsh glare. King Roland let out a nervous chuckle. The king was mighty, but his wife could control anyone with only a look. Queen Abry was a high-spirited woman, and King Roland had fallen in love with that aspect of her.

Adair tried not to gag as affection radiated from his parents' eyes. He was saved as a servant entered the room to inform everyone that the horses and the rest of the men were waiting at the castle's western gate.

Adair and Bennett quickly headed for the stables. The prince was passionate about hunting and he was ready to show his father that he could lead on his own.

When the duo arrived, the other men bowed as the prince entered.

"Good evening, Prince Adair," one man spoke.

Adair dipped his head in respect as he mounted his horse. "Good evening, gentlemen. Shall we go?"

The men cheered as Prince Adair led his horse from the western gate. They followed behind him, cheering for miles as they left the capital of Aria behind.

Adair looked back as the walls that surrounded Aria's capital shrunk with each trod of his horse. He smirked to himself. It was finally his day. There was a small village not far from the path they were on. If they needed more supplies, it would not be a long journey to get them. Slowly, Adair led his men off the path and toward the forest. He knew this hunting path by heart. He had hunted with his father and these men for as long as he could mount a horse.

As their horses raced through the forest, Adair heard something from the left. He raised a hand to silence and stop the group before dismounting his horse. He took the bow and an arrow from his supplies. Adair nocked the arrow and held it in place as he carefully walked to the left. That's when he saw it. A large buck stood grazing on the grass about thirty feet from them. Adair slowly lifted the bow. The rest of the men watched in awe, surprised that they had found a deer so quickly. Usually they were out for days tracking.

Adair let go of the arrow and watched as it sailed through the air. It pierced the deer in the backside. The animal cried out in pain before it darted off with an arrow sticking from its hide.

"Damn it," Adair cursed as he ran to remount his horse. He fumbled with the reins as he climbed. "Don't let it escape!" He called to his men as he urged his horse to race after the deer. His men followed behind obediently.

Chapter 2

Halona gave the tall, redheaded young man who stood in the doorway of the village medical hut a scolding look. His left arm was bleeding. He rubbed the back of his head sheepishly with his good arm as they stared at each other with matching green eyes.

"Evian." The name rolled from her tongue, causing her older brother to cringe. She motioned for him to sit on the cot beside her. He obeyed the small woman's orders and flinched when he saw her furious glare up close. She searched around in the cabinets of the hut before walking to her brother with a basket of supplies in her pale hands.

"You and Severin were training again." It was a statement, not a question. The harsh tone of her voice made Evian cringe once more.

He let out a nervous chuckle before speaking. "Yeah. We got a little carried away. You should see what he looks like."

"I'm assuming he doesn't have a single scratch. You can't beat him, Evian. He's a strong fighter." She gave her brother a teasing smirk as she began mixing herbs into a bowl to create a brown paste.

Evian sighed dejectedly before asking, "Where's Mariana?" He looked around the hut. The clan's healer was always in the medical hut. She rarely left her apprentice there alone.

"Father wanted to see her." Halona began to spread the paste onto the slice in her brother's arm. "You need to be more careful. This cut is deeper than the last one."

Evian hissed as the paste left a burning sensation in his flesh. He laughed to hide his pain from his sister. "I was only sparring with Severin. It's not like he would intentionally kill me."

13

Halona shot her brother a serious look. "He could if he wanted too. You're lucky he's more level-headed than the rest of us."

Evian hissed as the burning sensation grew. Halona slowly began applying bandages over the paste as it glowed a pale shade of green.

"Why does healing magic hurt so much?" Evian frowned once the burning ended.

"Because you are a wimp," Halona teased. "You're all set. Try to be more careful next time. I didn't use a lot of magic; it will need more time to heal. Don't go getting sliced up by Severin again."

"It's not my fault the man is always training," Evian groaned. "He needs to loosen up. He's just like Pops."

Halona rolled her eyes as she began putting the supplies away. Evian stood to help her put everything back where it belonged. He pulled the bloody sheets from the cot and tossed them into a basket of dirty laundry in the corner.

"How is it having the whole medical hut to yourself? You feel like a real healer yet?" He smiled in Halona's direction.

She frowned and put her hands on her hips. "For your information, I am a real healer!"

Evian held his hands up in defense to protect himself from the tiny girl's wrath. "I didn't mean to offend you! I was just wondering since you're still Mariana's apprentice."

Halona sighed as she put fresh sheets onto the cot. "Sorry, I've just been on edge since I had that meeting with Seyu the other day."

Evian nodded. "That's right. Seyu and his prophecy talk. It's a bunch of hoo-ha." He waved his hands in the air dramatically.

Halona punched him in his good arm, "Shut up, Moron. I believe in it. I'm supposed to meet the other Peace Bringer soon."

"Our clan is already at peace. The Avory haven't had an incident with Aria in years. You can't bring peace when it already exists."

Halona rolled her eyes again. Her brother would never learn. He might not believe in the Prophecy foretold by her destiny mark, and that was fine. She believed. Just as their mother had believed.

Once the sheets were on the cot, she began to complete the list of tasks that Mariana had given her before she left. Most of them were simple cleaning or organizing tasks. Others were practicing on healing and magic control. One task was to remember to eat. Halona was always getting so engrossed in her duties that she forgot to feed herself. And a given, of course, was to heal any injury that Evian came in with.

Halona chuckled as she went to retrieve her lunch from the back room. She inhaled a small sandwich made of tomato and a slice of lamb before crossing eating and healing Evian off the list. She decided the cleaning tasks would be next because the sun had not set yet.

Evian remained to keep his little sister company.

The healer, Mariana, returned just as Halona was starting on the windows. Mariana was much older than Halona. Her blonde hair was aged gray. She was the Avory clan's best and only healer. She had taken Halona under her wing years before as a promise to the girl's mother.

"Welcome back." Halona smiled at the woman.

Mariana returned the smile. "How was your afternoon, Princess?"

Halona's eyes rolled at Mariana's respectfulness. "How many times do I have to tell you not to call me that? Mariana, you're my teacher."

Mariana gave the girl a devious smirk. "I am aware. I do it because you hate it."

Halona sighed and gave her teacher a small nudge. "You're mad."

Mariana laughed and finished helping the girl with her tasks. Evian tried to help, but Mariana kept shooing him out of her way with the excuse that it was healer's work. She wanted to keep him from touching anything after the broken vial of potion he had been responsible for the week before. Evian patiently sat on a cot and waited for his sister to finish her duties for the day.

"Are you almost done yet?" Evian occasionally whined just to get on Halona's nerves. She threw something at him every time he complained. Mariana laughed at the siblings' banter. She had helped their mother, Elexia, birth each of her four children. A sad smile crossed Mariana's face as she watched the two youngest children of her best friend.

"You two are so much like your mother," she said with a quiet laugh. The duo paused their bickering to smile and laugh at Mariana. They were always being told that they were spitting images of their late mother, and they felt honored that she was remembered so fondly.

It did not take long for the duo to finish cleaning the hut. Evian slumped against the far wall and dramatically sighed.

"That was tiring," he panted.

Halona smacked him upside the head with a laugh, "You barely did anything, Stupid."

Evian rubbed the back of his head as Mariana began ushering them out the door. "You two go home. It's late. I'm sure your father is expecting you. His council meeting should be over soon."

The siblings opened their mouths to retort, but before they could say anything, Mariana shut the door in their faces. Evian laughed and commented on the older woman's impatience. Halona did not respond. She stood next to her brother, staring off into the distance.

Evian waved his hand in front of her face to get her attention. She did not budge, so he grabbed her by the shoulders and shook her.

"Halona!"

She snapped out of her trance and shook her head. She gave Evian an apologetic smile before pointing toward the forest in the direction she had been staring.

"I saw a few men go that way with weapons. We just went hunting. No one is allowed to go out on their own." She started walking in the direction she had pointed. Evian called after her, telling her that she was probably just crazy, but Halona knew what she saw. She knew the rules of the village, but her curious nature was getting the better of her.

Evian groaned before grabbing her arm to stop her, "If you're going to follow, we need to take our own weapons. It could be dangerous."

She looked toward the forest and then nodded to her brother. They could sneak back into their house to retrieve their own weapons without their father knowing. The weekly council meeting was still in session.

Chapter 3

Prince Adair looked around for his kill, his blue eyes scanning the surroundings. He and the rest of Aria's Royal hunters had been out all day looking for the deer Adair had shot. It was getting late and Adair was about ready to call it quits. They had chased the injured animal far off the path. Nothing looked familiar.

When the prince finally spotted the injured deer, he shot it again with his arrow. He saw it drop, but when he went to retrieve it, it was gone.

"Adair, I don't want to be rude, but are you positive that you actually took down the animal?" Bennett came alongside him. Adair could sense the humor in his friend's voice.

Adair gave his friend a quick nod and a chuckle, "Of course I shot the damn deer, Bennett. You watched it drop." He gave a quick, irritated glance toward the man. "I also distinctly remember you commenting on the sloppiness of my shot, but the look on your face when the animal fell was priceless."

Bennett laughed and shook his head at the prince as he joked. "True, but I could have imagined the whole thing. You never have been very skilled with a bow."

Adair briefly stopped his search and smirked at Bennett. "Marriage is affecting your brain, my friend," he joked, earning another laugh from the man.

"That is just another excuse for you to remain a bachelor," Bennett laughed, shaking his head.

Adair resumed his search for the deer, eventually finding the buck's half-eaten carcass in a bush.

"Damn it," he swore under his breath. Bennett appeared at his side and looked down at the carcass.

"It seems something beat us to our trophy," Bennett said with a sigh.

Adair shook his head, upset. Bennett placed a hand on the young man's shoulder. "We can't win them all."

Adair grumbled under his breath and shrugged Bennett's hand off his shoulder.

A few of the other men joined them.

"Prince Adair, do you want to head back to the palace?" one asked. "We have strayed far off our usual hunting path. It will take us time to return to the right path. I suggest we head back now."

The prince groaned in annoyance and shot the man a glare. He usually kept to himself at the palace, always studying or training with his sword. He always tried to keep his emotions in check, but this hunt was making it more difficult by the minute.

"If you want to return now, be my guest. I am not going back to the palace until I have a trophy," he addressed his men.

"Adair, your parents would have our heads if we returned without you. We can try again tomorrow on our way back to the palace, but we really should rest," Bennett protested. He shivered at the thought of Queen Abry's wrath.

The prince sighed and considered his friend's words. "Very well."

Bennett smiled and patted the prince's back before going to talk to the other men in the hunting party as they began to set up camp. Adair's head shot up when he heard one of his men shout in terror.

Adair searched for the frightened man. Eventually, he found him on the ground, shaking with fear. Adair's eyes widened when he saw what had frightened the man. In front of them stood a large wooden stake. On the tip of the stake was a severed human head.

The head was scalped clean of all hair with eyes protruding from the sockets and the mouth hanging open. The tongue had been cut out, and a mass of maggots rested inside the open mouth. Adair gagged from the wretched stench as he covered his mouth and nose.

"We're in savage territory," he whispered as he scrambled back to the rest of the men.

Bennett saw the concern on the young prince's face. "Adair, is everything alright?"

Adair shook his head violently, "No, we've landed ourselves in savage territory. We need to go. Now."

Gasps could be heard from the men as they began packing their supplies and mounting their horses.

Adair looked around, frantic. He had no idea where they were or how to get back to Aria's lands. They were not safe in here. If they were found, they were dead, and there would be nothing left of them to return to their families.

As their horses bolted, Adair had a sneaking suspicion that they were being followed.

◇•◇•◇

Three young, savage men had been following the tracks of the Aria hunters for hours and were waiting for the right moment to strike. The leader of the group smirked. His shaggy, brown hair fell over his blue eyes that gleamed under the moonlight with a sick and sadistic glint.

The savage's two lackeys stood behind him with similar sadistic smirks. The tallest in the group held an axe. He was skinny, but quick on his feet. His green eyes were filled with mischief. His hair was black. The last man was the shortest and ugliest of the group. His eyes were a dull brown and his wiry blond hair was pulled back into a low ponytail.

The three began making their way toward the group of fleeing Arian men when they stopped in their tracks. An arrow bore into a tree branch just above the leader's head.

He chuckled darkly as he turned around and said, "Hello, Halona."

In the moonlight, Halona stood with her bow and arrow in her hands. She had another arrow nocked and was ready to fire if necessary. Evian stood beside her with his sword.

"Mind telling us what you three are up to, Eagon?" Evian pointed the sword in the group's direction.

The leader, Eagon, laughed, "We're just dealing with some pests that entered into Avory territory."

The tall man spoke next, "Yeah, I saw the Arian crest on their uniforms and horses. No doubt that their heads will fetch us quite the profit when the Mercants come through for trading season."

Halona scoffed and pulled her arrow back. "You three are disgusting."

The ugly one spoke up. "They're in our territory. They know better than to show up here."

Eagon nodded and laughed, dismissing the siblings with a jerk of his chin. "Let's go boys. We don't want to associate ourselves with trash. I don't understand why their father keeps them around. Useless."

"Why you little . . ." Halona growled as she made a move to fire her arrow. The taller savage moved at a hasty pace. He got around the girl and twisted her arm behind her back. Halona yelped in pain as she dropped her bow. She heard cracking sounds as her shoulder dislocated. The savage pushed her onto her knees and held her in place. Evian brought his sword up to help his sister, only to have it kicked from his hand by Eagon's ugly henchman. His foot connected with Evian's gut, causing the redhaired man to drop to the ground coughing.

Eagon chuckled once more as he approached the siblings. He bent down and reached for Halona, tilting her chin up. "It's a shame that a pretty girl like you is so stupid."

Halona pulled her face from his hand and spit in his eye. Eagon frowned at her and pulled a dagger from his belt.

"Little whore," he hissed as he brought the blade down. It sliced through her tunic and cut into her side. Halona screeched in pain; the sound rippled through the still air of the forest.

dair's head snapped in the direction of the scream. Assuming he was hearing a savage battle cry, he imagined the high-pitched sound filled with the pain of the savages' victims. Frightened, he kept leading his men in the direction he believed was away from savage territory. He had no idea where he was going. He could only assume, by the mounting numbers of severed heads, that they were getting close to the edge of the territory.

Behind him, one of Adair's men let out a garbled sound. Adair turned around just in time to see the man fall off his horse. A small axe protruded from the man's back. The man's horse kicked and stomped before running off into the forest. When the dust settled, there was nothing left that resembled the man.

"They found us!" The other men shouted. Their horses started to get anxious. Another axe flew from the bushes and buried into the side of Adair's horse. The horse whinnied and kicked the young prince off its back before running away. Around Adair, horses and men were panicking. More men dropped as arrows and axes hit their bodies. Some injured men managed to escape into the forest, but it was possible that more savages were waiting there for them. Bennett reached down to help the prince onto his horse. Another man dropped off his horse as an axe was embedded into his head.

"Filthy savages," Bennett mumbled under his breath. Soon, Eagon and his men stepped from the shadows of the forest.

"Well, it seems we have visitors." Eagon laughed.

Adair unsheathed his sword and pointed it at the savages.

Bennett held up his hand to the prince. "Let me handle this," Bennett whispered.

"Are you mad? They are savages. They can't be reasoned with," Adair hissed with scowl.

Bennett held his hands up toward the savages. He stepped down from the horse and looked at his friend. Adair's eyes widened. Bennett was going to stall them so Adair could escape.

Adair shook his head at his friend, a silent order to return to the horse.

"We strayed from our normal hunting path. We had no ill intentions when coming into your territory. If you let us go, we'll be on our way without further incident," Bennett said, turning his back on the prince.

Eagon laughed and stepped toward the man. "You expect us to just let you go? You've made it further into our territory than you think. Besides, a catch like the Arian Royal Hunt could fetch us a lot of money."

Bennett opened his mouth to speak again, but was interrupted by Eagon's sword as it was pushed through his chest. Adair stared in horror as his best friend's body slumped to the ground in a pool of blood.

"Bennett!" The prince shrieked.

Eagon gave the young man a smirk as he stepped toward the prince. Adair grabbed the reigns of Bennett's horse and sped off through the forest. As he rode away, thoughts flooded his mind. Bennett could not be dead. He had a wife and a child on the way. Adair had known Bennett for practically all his life. He was not dead. It was impossible.

Adair heard Eagon swear from behind as the trio chased him.

That's when he saw her.

A savage woman stood on a large branch of tree just ahead of him. As their eyes met, he felt the pain that was reflected in her face. She held up a bow and pointed it at Adair. Her white shirt was stained red with blood. She wore a vest of fur over the bloody shirt.

"Duck!" The savage female yelled as the prince rode closer. He didn't know who she was talking to, but he lowered his body against the horse's back. Her arrow whizzed over his head and he heard a groan from behind. He turned and saw the ugly henchman's body drop to the ground. An arrow protruded from his head.

"Aron!" The tall lackey shouted as he ran to the shorter man's body. He noticed the girl in the tree and shouted at her, "Halona!"

Adair watched as the woman fired another arrow into the tall man's shoulder.

The savage grabbed his shoulder in pain and shouted another string of curses at the girl.

Adair took the man's distraction as an opportunity to attack. He turned the horse around and ran right for the taller henchman. He heard the girl shout something from behind him, but he did not care. He wanted revenge for his fallen comrades. He swung his sword as he reached the man. As Adair rode past, he watched as the man's head slid off his shoulders.

The woman began screeching at him again. He turned to her and shouted back. "Shut up you savage wench."

The woman's face flushed red in anger. "Don't call me a wench! I should just let Eagon kill you if you're going to be an asshole."

She put her bow onto her back and sat on the branch. Breathing heavily, she rested her back against the tree. She tore off an already ripped piece of her shirt, revealing a bloody gash in her side. She placed her hands over her side and they began to glow green.

Adair watched with his sword drawn. He kept an eye on her, hoping to anticipate her next move. Savages were known to take kills from each other. Perhaps this woman's goal was to let him finish off the others before she would finish him off. He was ready to attack should this woman come after him. As he watched her closely, he saw her eyes widened and she began to point at something behind him. She was not going to attack him? Puzzled, he began to take several steps back while her attention was elsewhere.

Adair heard a shout from behind. He saw Eagon running toward him with his sword drawn. Jumping out of the way at the last moment, he mentally thanked whatever deity was looking out for him before he swung his own sword at the savage man. The sword sliced into Eagon's arm. It embedded deep in the bone, causing the arm to fall limply to the savage's side. Eagon groaned in pain and sloppily swung his sword into Adair's left shoulder.

Adair hissed and moved his sword to his other hand. He swung in Eagon's direction. The swing from his non-dominant hand was sloppy. He missed and lost his balance, causing him to fall to the ground and land on his injured shoulder. He let out a pain-filled cry as Eagon laughed maniacally, stepping toward the prince. The savage raised his sword to bring it down into the prince's chest. Time moved in slow-motion as Adair waited for the pain and then his death. Memories of his mother, father, Bennett, and Alicia flooded his mind. This was it. This was the end.

"You'll make a fine king one day, my son," he heard his father say.

"You look dashing this evening, Adair," his mother gushed.

"You'll have to marry eventually. It isn't so bad. Look at Alicia and me. We couldn't be happier." Bennett's voice echoed through his mind.

Before the sword could pierce Adair's skin, Eagon's eyes widened. Blood poured from his mouth and his body slumped to the side. Adair's vision began to fade as he lost more blood from his shoulder wound. He watched, helpless, as a large figure stood where Eagon had been standing. A bloody sword rested in the figure's hands. The figure spoke, but Adair could not understand a word as he slipped into darkness. Before he fell completely out of consciousness, he saw a second figure join the first.

Halona slowly descended from the tree. She had returned her shoulder to the socket, but the gash in her side refused to stop bleeding. She wrapped a cloth around it to try to slow it. She held her injured side once she was on the ground. Blood had seeped through most of her shirt. She wheezed as she tried to remain conscious. Her adrenaline had helped her before, but now she could feel herself growing weaker. She looked toward the figure in the shadows.

"Father." She hung her head, believing that she was in trouble. Evian stepped from the shadows and stood next to their father.

"Halona," Roka said as he stood towering over his youngest child. His bushy beard moved as he talked. "I heard your scream from the village. I found Evian while I was looking for you. He led me here. Let me look at your injuries."

The man stepped toward her and lifted her shirt to inspect her side. He carefully scooped his daughter up into his arms. As he picked her up, she saw the familiar mark on Adair's forehead.

"Father, wait!" she yelled, astonished. She pointed down to Adair's unconscious form. "Look at his forehead."

Roka stared down at the Prince of Aria. His eyes widened. He handed his daughter to her brother and reached down for the prince. Throwing the young man over his shoulder, the Avory chief headed toward his village.

Chapter 4

others have a sixth sense. They know when their children are in danger. Queen Abry learned early in her son's life that she had this ability when he was just a small child and had fallen out of a tree.

Queen Abry stood on the balcony outside the bedroom she shared with her husband. She was having that feeling again as she stared toward the west. Her features were etched with worry and her hands trembled. She had to place them on the railing to prevent herself from falling.

She heard a door open from behind, but she never turned away from the west. She knew it was her husband. It was too late for servants to enter.

"Adair will be fine, Love. I am confident in him," Roland whispered as he leaned toward her ear. His arms circled her waist and brought her close to him. He held his wife as he had many times before, to end her worrying.

"I have a terrible feeling in the pit of my stomach," Abry let out a sigh and leaned her head back onto her husband's shoulder. King Roland continued to reassure his wife that their only son would be fine on his journey. She could not let go of the terrible feeling that her son was in danger. Her motherly instincts were telling her to protect him, but he was miles away. She could only hope that her instincts were wrong for once.

King Roland tried ushering Queen Abry into bed, but she refused to budge. He kissed her head before heading back into the castle to go sleep. Queen Abry's eyes never left the west. She stood on the balcony watching until the sun rose in the east.

◊ • ◊ • ◊

Chapter 5

dair felt something cold on his face. His eyes slowly opened and he saw a girl sitting beside him. He could not recall meeting this girl before, but he figured he was at home in the palace. He thought she was one of the palace servants. It was then that Adair realized he was on a cot and not his bed at the palace. He glanced down to see his bandaged chest and injured shoulder.

Slowly, images from the previous night began to flood his mind. His eyes widened as he remembered. He looked into the girl's eyes. The jade color seemed familiar. He started to scramble away from her, only to have a searing pain ripple through his upper body.

"Relax, I won't hurt you. I'm glad you're awake. You've been out cold for almost three days." The young woman dabbed a wet cloth on his forehead and spoke softly in a way that was clearly meant to calm Adair's nerves.

He kept his guard up. The young prince took in the girl's features. She appeared to be around the same age as him, but she was much smaller than he originally thought. He remembered her large, green eyes from the other night, but he had not noticed the bright red hair framing her face. He saw dangling earrings made from bone. A similar necklace rested around her neck. Her brown shirt stopped at her midriff, revealing bandages covering her side. He tried to recall her name. Something told him that it started with an *H*. He rattled through as many *H* names as he could before he gave up, unable to find the girl's name in his memory.

"Why help me if you *savages* killed my hunting party." He choked out the words as he felt tears begin to sting his eyes. He could not bring himself to believe Bennett was gone. He half expected his friend to be laying in a cot somewhere in this godforsaken hut, but he was not. Adair's hands began to shake as he put them to his face.

"You killed them," he whispered as he looked up at her with a glare.

She frowned and pointed a finger at him. He noticed her nails were longer and sharper than any woman he had ever met. He inwardly shivered at the thought of her ripping him apart, using those deadly claws of hers.

"First off," she began as she jabbed her finger into his face. "I did not kill your friends. Eagon, Aron, and Erwyn are the ones who killed them. And if I remember correctly, *you* killed Erwyn. I hardly believe you're in any position to blame me when I am the one who saved your ass."

Adair frowned at the woman. He groaned and gripped his shoulder when the pain returned. She handed him a wooden cup with a floral design carved into the rim. Inside the cup was a thick, brown liquid.

"Drink. It'll temporarily relieve your pain and speed up your body's healing."

The prince stared at her for a moment. Could he really trust this girl? He had watched Bennett and the rest of his men die at the hands of these filthy savages.

"Oh please, if I had wanted to kill you, I would have already done it. You aren't exactly in any condition to defend yourself," she said as she folded her arms and growled as if she was offended.

"Why help me if your comrades attacked me? I thought your tribes were everything to you savages." Prince Adair had to take a deep breath to keep his thoughts away from the pain in his upper body.

"First, it is a clan, not a tribe. Second, we prefer to be called *barbarians*," she said.

Adair could not tell if she was kidding about wanting to be called a barbarian as opposed to a savage. He saw no difference between the words.

"Third," she continued to speak. "I never really got along with those three. Not to mention, Eagon gave me this." She pointed to the wound on her side. "They might have been killed anyway for attacking my brother and me. You saved us the trouble of killing all of them."

She placed her hand on his and pushed the drink closer to his mouth. "Now drink from this damned cup before I force it down your throat."

This savage woman treated him with such disrespect. It was infuriating. Adair took the cup and sipped it slowly. There was a grainy texture to the thick concoction. Once he swallowed, the liquid burned as it went down, causing him to gag. The girl's eyes rolled as she tilted the cup up so all the liquid ran down his throat.

He swallowed and began coughing, which worsened the pain in his chest. "Are you mad?" he hissed, once he was done coughing. He began to survey his surroundings. From the looks of it, he was in a small hut. Light shined through the two windows, so he assumed it was morning.

The girl rolled her eyes again. "It will only work to numb your pain if you drink all of it."

Before he could speak again, an older woman walked into the hut. She walked over to the pair and smiled. "Princess Halona, how is our friend doing?"

Adair glared at the woman. She either did not notice or did not care.

Halona was the girl's name. Adair remembered it now. He felt a slight tinge of satisfaction at realizing her name after his struggle recalling it. He glanced up, confused that she was given the title princess. This girl could not possibly be nobility. The clothes she wore resembled rags, and her pale skin was filthy. He tuned into the conversation to gain more information.

"He is doing well, Mariana. If I can get him to drink the herbs, he should be better in a few weeks. I infused a little more magic than normal into the drink like you showed me. Hopefully, that will help him heal faster." Halona spoke as if Adair was not in the room.

The older woman nodded, her gray curls flopping up and down. "Your father wanted to come in to visit with you and our friend," she said, and gestured toward Adair.

Adair huffed silently. "I have a name."

Mariana gave him a smile that was sickly sweet. "Of course, you do, dear." She left the hut, chuckling to herself.

Adair looked at the girl as she picked at the bandages on her side. He was about to tell her not to pick at them or she would not heal, but a dim light covered her hand. She slowly unwrapped the bandages as the light glowed. What he saw was astonishing. Her skin was slowly healing itself. It was miniscule, but Adair could see the skin repairing.

She noticed his astonishment and smiled. "I'm a healer. I use magic and herbs to heal wounds. I'm still learning. My magic is not as strong as Mariana's."

He looked at her, puzzled. "Magic is illegal and punishable by death," he said.

She let out a soft and melodic laugh as she began to redress her wound.

"Maybe in your country, but here we use a type of fire magic to heal the sick and injured. Let me guess," she continued with a laugh. "You don't believe in fate or destiny either."

His blank expression was the answer to her question. Her mouth dropped open, flabbergasted. "How? I mean, you have a destiny mark!" She pointed to the small diamond mark on his forehead.

He groaned. Great, not only was he trapped here, but the girl caring for him was just as insane as Eyra.

"Destiny, fate, and prophecies are a bunch of boarshit," he said with a shake of his head. Halona continued to stare at him in bewilderment.

The door to the hut flew open and Roka entered. Adair's eyes widened at the size of him. The man's long, dark brown hair was pulled back. His thick beard appeared to be trimmed. The man's clothing was nothing compared to anything Adair and his father wore, but it was superior to the clothing Halona wore. The man's cobalt eyes stared down at Adair with an intimidating force. Adair felt like the man was looking into his soul. He shifted uncomfortably in the cot he was on and was surprised when he hardly noticed the pain from before.

Halona had risen to her feet when her father entered the hut. She kept her eyes cast down. Adair watched her from the corner of his eye as she picked at the patches sewn into her brown pants.

"Halona." The intimidating man tore his eyes away from Adair to look at his daughter. She let out a small squeak and looked up at him.

"Yes, Father?"

He strutted over to Halona and began inspecting her side. "How are you feeling?" He put a gentle and comforting hand on her shoulder.

She nodded and gave her father a warm smile. Her shyness was slowly beginning to disappear. "I'm fine, Father."

He nodded before turning back to Adair. The young prince gulped and looked down at his hands to focus on something else. Not only was Roka's stature and build intimidating, but he seemed to emit a dangerous aura from the way he carried himself. Adair tried hiding his fear as a large, pale hand landed on his forehead and pushed him back into the pillow.

"What is your name, boy?" Halona's father snarled. His teeth were sharpened and his nails were also filed to dangerously sharp points.

"My name is Adair," he spoke slowly. "Prince of Aria." He added the rest of his title to show that he was special. If these savages killed or harmed him, they would have the Arian army at their doorstep.

The leader released Adair's head and looked at Halona. He motioned for her to walk with him to the back of the hut and the two spoke for several minutes. Adair lay on the cot and watched them speak, but could not make out a word they were saying because it seemed to be in another language.

It felt like an eternity when they finally returned to Adair's bedside. Halona sat in chair while her father towered above them. The man addressed Adair. "I cannot allow you to return to your home for the safety of my clan. You understand my situation?"

Adair said nothing as he glared at the savage man. A small smirk appeared on the leader's face. "I was going to leave you to die in the forest. However, you have a destiny mark. Seeing how my daughter is also a Peace Bringer, I have allowed you to live. You will become the servant of Halona when you are healed. Anything she tells you to do, you do it. You are no longer a prince and will not act as such. Understood?"

"Servant?" Adair scoffed which earned him a snarl from Roka. The prince could not keep his body from flinching at the sight of the man's pointed teeth.

"If you refuse this offer, I can always just kill you now."

Adair frowned. "No, you won't. You need me."

Roka frowned and, in one swift motion, had a dagger to Adair's throat. "My daughter doesn't need you to help her. If you die, there is still another Peace Bringer left to fulfill the prophecy. Do you understand me?"

Adair's eyes widened as he felt at the shining metal blade touching his throat. Roka was not pushing hard, but it was enough for a few drops of blood to trickle down Adair's neck.

"Yes," Adair spoke quietly. He could not hide the fear in his voice, which made Roka smirk.

"Very well," Roka said, turning to Halona. "He is your responsibility now. I suggest you keep an eye on him."

She nodded and watched as her father left the hut. She noticed Adair glare behind her father's back as he walked out. Halona released a breath that she had been holding and sat back in her chair.

Adair groaned once more. "How have I managed to go from being a prince to a lowly servant? I refuse to act as such. It's beneath me."

Halona raised an eyebrow and looked at her new servant. "You really aren't in a position to complain. There are plenty of people here who would love to use you as target practice, myself included, you pompous fool."

"Then why not kill me if you feel that way? Kill me like your kind did to the rest of my hunting party. Kill me just like you bastards killed Bennett." Adair challenged the girl. He could see his sword leaning against the far wall. He thought he could easily kill the girl if she tried anything.

"Again, I did not kill them. I don't want to kill you. You have a destiny mark. You are important." She shrugged and flicked the diamond birthmark on his forehead. Up close, Adair could finally see the minute, brown diamond mark on her neck. He gave her an unconvinced look and glanced again at his sword.

"You are far more injured than I am," she said as she walked to his equipment and picked it up. "Attacking me will only get you injured more."

She took the sword and armor to the backroom before returning to the main room. She busied herself at a workstation by grinding herbs into a paste.

"Why were you out in the forest anyway? There aren't many people from your country who venture into the Avory's neck of the woods. Were you coming to attack us?"

She said the last part in a soft and sad voice.

Adair narrowed his eyes. "You are the ones who attacked us! We were only trying to hunt."

Halona sighed a breath of relief.

"I'm sorry about the attack," she said.

"I don't need your pity," Adair snapped bitterly.

She raised an eyebrow at him and shrugged. "You're not the only one who has lost someone close to you. The world doesn't revolve around you. Just remember that you are my . . ."

He cut her off before she could finish. "Do not say it! I refuse to be a servant. I would rather die a prince than live my life as a servant. Especially as a servant to a savage like you."

Halona stared at the blue-eyed man. "We are not savages. This clan is the Avory. I suggest that you use that name. I thought pride was considered a sin to your people?"

Adair could not tell if she was serious or mocking him.

"Shut up," he spat irritably.

Halona let out a giggle. "I wonder how far I until I push you to your limit?" She poked the diamond on his forehead.

"Try it and I will kill you, Wench." Adair reached up to grab her hand. They both knew it was an empty threat. Adair was too injured to harm the girl. He let go of her hand and groaned. "I still don't understand why I must serve you now. You should be serving me. My father is King of Aria."

He heard the girl laugh again. "It was fate," she spoke softly.

His eyes glanced in her direction. "As I said before, fate is boarshit. You expect me to believe that I lost my men because the universe wanted them to die? Why would you believe something so atrocious? It's disgusting."

Halona's emerald eyes rolled again as she began explaining the concept of fate.

"The Avory, and most of the other clans, believe in fate. It is a concept given to us by the moon. Every life has meaning even long before they are born. When it is time to die, you die. It's as simple as that. We cannot control life, and we cannot prevent death. We are here to fulfill our purpose, and then we leave this world."

Adair did not want to listen to her boring lecture, and he did not have to for long. He fell asleep, too tired to listen to her speak as if she was reciting from a book.

Halona noticed the prince had fallen asleep. She laughed to herself and stood, stretching her legs. She glanced back to the prince and pulled a blanket over his body. The weather had gotten warmer since winter ended, but the spring nights were still chilly.

There was a knock at the door and Evian stood there with his signature goofy grin. "Mariana is almost done with dinner. It's time to go home. He'll be fine. Father has already instructed everyone that he is not to be harmed. Let's go. You look like you could use some meat on your bones," he said before walking and poking his sister in the ribs on her uninjured side.

Halona frowned. Evian always made fun of how small she was. Her brothers always called her the "runt of the litter."

"Shut up, Moron," she said and smacked his hand away. "I'll be home in a little while."

Evian nodded before waving goodbye and exiting the hut. Halona sighed with a frown as her stomach growled. She grabbed a piece of paper and a quill, wrote a quick note to the prince, and left it on the chair next to his cot. She filled the wooden cup with more of the herb drink and placed it by the note before leaving the medical hut. She took a deep breath as she slowly walked down the street of the small village.

Halona smiled as she breathed in the spring air. She could faintly smell bread being baked somewhere in the village. Huts were all around her. Many were small homes for the families living in the village. Others were shops, weaponries, or storehouses. The village's assembly hut was the biggest building in town. It had to hold as many people from the village as possible. This was usually where her father delivered important speeches or where ceremonies took place. Sometimes, weddings took place inside if the weather did not permit an outdoor ceremony.

Halona grinned as the smell of meat filled her nose when she got closer. As it was the third night of the week, she should have been the one to cook for her father and brothers. The family took turns making meals throughout the week. Mariana and the others had tried to teach Halona all the skills she needed to be a decent cook, but none of their lessons seemed to stick with her. She was terrible at cooking and her family never wanted to eat anything she prepared. Mariana had taken Halona's night to cook.

Halona stepped through the doors to her home and smiled widely at the smell of meat and potatoes. Her stomached rumbled.

"I heard Father is letting you keep a prince for a pet," a voice came from further inside the main room of the hut. She saw her eldest brother, Liam, resting in one of the chairs. His feet were in the air and his head was toward the floor.

Her eyes rolled. "Only because he's the other Peace Bringer."

"I still don't understand why we have Peace Bringers when there is already peace," Evian said with a groan as he flopped into another chair.

A third voice entered the conversation with a serious tone. "We could be close to another war. Our lands are in the heart of Aria, and if they learn that we have their prince, it will get ugly."

Halona's head snapped in the direction of the voice. She saw Liam's younger twin, Severin, sitting in another chair on the opposite side of the room. His nose was in a book and he was not looking at anyone.

"Don't be so serious, Severin." Liam shook his head as he tossed a pebble. They may have been twins, but telling them apart was easy. Liam chose to keep his short red hair spiked neatly on top of his head. Severin opted for a flatter look and sported a bushy beard. Liam was much skinnier than his younger twin. Severin was bulkier from the amount of training he constantly put his body through.

Halona nodded. "Severin is right. Why would there be a prophecy about Peace Bringers if peace already existed? Something has to be going on in Aria or somewhere else."

"Another clan could also attack us. We haven't been attacked since . . ." Severin never finished his sentence. They all knew what he was going to say.

"Yeah, it's still hard to believe it's been that long since she died." Liam's normally cheerful face took on a solemn look. Evian and Halona nodded in agreement.

Mariana stepped into the main room of the family's hut. She could tell something was bothering the siblings, but she did not question it. Her intuition filled in the blanks.

"Dinner's ready," she said and smiled, ushering them all into the dining area. Roka was nowhere to be found.

"Is Pops missing dinner again?" Evian looked around.

Halona rolled her eyes at Evian.

Mariana nodded. "He asked if you would save him a plate for when he returns. He had some clan business to take care of with his advisors."

Halona sighed. "He's overdoing it again. We all know he won't be back until morning."

"He's not overdoing it, Halona," Severin said, glancing her way. "He has a village to run and people to protect."

Liam nodded. "True, but he does go overboard. The village is safe. If I ever get to be that bad when I'm leading, knock some sense into me. Keeping the village safe is important, but so is spending time with your family."

"I could knock some sense into you now," Halona suggested, throwing a slice of potato at Liam. It hit his cheek and dropped onto his plate.

"I'm being serious," Liam said with an uncharacteristic frown.

Halona nodded, knowing Liam was right. Their father was always one who put his clan before anything else. They were his people, and he was constantly making decisions to keep his people alive and well. Perhaps he was going overboard, but after the events of the last attack, his actions were justified.

Chapter 6

dair woke from his nap in a sweat. He was breathing heavy. Bennett's death kept replaying over and over in his dreams. He sat up, looking for Halona around the medical hut, but he could not find her. He noticed a note in the chair beside him and reached out to grab it once his breathing returned to normal. He hissed in pain as he reached. The movement stretched his sore muscles, causing them to protest.

Adair,

It is time for my family to eat dinner together. I would have woken you, but until you are healed, I will have to bring you food after I finish my meals. Don't worry; I will feed you!

Do not try to escape. We have scouts outside and inside the village. If you try to leave, they will kill you and I cannot do anything about that. Please, stay put. If you get bored, feel free to look around the hut. I brought in some books for you to read. They are written in the ancient Avory language, but they have some great pictures! Drink from the wooden cup. I know the herbs taste terrible, but they will help you heal faster and take care of your pain.

Halona

Adair stared at the note and sighed. He had hoped that he would find a quick escape and get back to Aria, but that was starting to seem impossible. He glanced into the wooden cup at the brownish green mixture and inwardly gagged. The liquid was thick and smelled like rotting flesh.

"I cannot believe I have to drink this shit," he mumbled as he took a sip. The burning sensation in his throat was back, but he remembered how well the drink had worked at taking away his pain. Quickly, he squeezed his nose with his fingers and in two large gulps, the drink was gone.

Images of Bennett's dead body flashed through his mind again. Adair shook his head and looked over at the books that Halona had left for him. Perhaps those would distract him. He knew trying to escape was futile. He was injured and, even though he could walk, he would not make it far before he was caught by the clan's warriors or an animal.

He waited several minutes for the pain in his chest to subside before he stood. He had to wait several moments more for the room to stop spinning. His pain may have been gone, but his body was still weak. He slowly hobbled to the stack of books and began to look through them. He started with the one on top and worked his way to the bottom.

He realized that Halona was telling the truth. The books were in a language he could not understand, but the artistry was phenomenal. He flipped through the pages and looked at the pictures. He stopped to stare at one picture. It was a map, but not any map he had ever seen. He recognized the outline of Salacir and the outlines of Aria, Etras, and Uron, but there were countless more borders throughout the countries. He remembered learning from a tutor that some of these borders belonged to savage tribes. He recognized the outline of the savage lands he was currently residing in. He could not make out the words on the page or the names of anything listed. He tore a corner off the note Halona had left him and marked his place in the book. He replaced it on the top of the stack and retreated to his cot. As he was pulling the blanket back over his legs, the door to the hut opened.

"Good, you are awake. I thought I was going to have to dump a bucket of water on you," Halona said with a laugh. She held a plate of delicious looking food in her hands. She returned to her seat by his cot and handed him the plate.

Adair's stomach growled. He had not known he was hungry until the smell of the food filled his nostrils.

"I see you drank all of the herb juice I left for you." Halona smiled as she picked up the empty wooden cup.

Adair's nose crinkled causing the woman to laugh. "Does it have to be so vile?" He asked.

"The herbs the drink is made from are not meant to be tasty. They're meant to heal and relieve pain. I suppose I could ask Mariana if there's a way to sweeten the bitter taste without ruining the healing properties."

Adair sniffed the plate of food. He glanced at Halona and then looked back at the food before taking a small bite. He instantly recognized the taste of the meat. It was boar. The food was nothing as extravagant as the food he ate daily, but it was delicious. He could taste hints of garlic and other spices. Adair continued to eat the food, but he did not thank her. "If I must stay here against my will, I would rather be treated like a human being and not an animal."

Halona glanced at him from the corner of her eye. "You do realize that your people think my people act like wild animals."

Adair glared at the girl, "You know what I mean, Girl."

Her eyebrow raised again, "I have a name. I suggest you use it. I'm trying to be nice to you and you're making it very difficult."

"I do not need you to be nice to me. I am Prince of Aria. You will treat me with respect and dignity," he grumbled.

"You don't deserve respect or dignity. How could you be the other Peace Bringer? You are so aggravating," she spat.

"Because destiny and fate are not real," he protested. "I don't care if you believe you are a Peace Bringer. You are not royalty, or even a trusted subject of the crown, therefore, you do not and will not have my respect."

She leaned forward and hissed bitterly, "And here in the Avory Clan, you are a prisoner. I will not recognize you as a prince."

Adair scoffed, but he stayed silent. Halona pulled a basket from one of the large crates sitting on the floor. She began making a paste from several herbs on the table. "I'm going to need you to stay sitting up. I need to change your bandages and heal your wound a little."

Adair groaned at the abrupt end to their argument. He had not won, but he did have the energy to continue. As well, he feared infection. He complied with Halona's request. She took the paste and the basket and sat in the chair beside Adair's cot. She carefully used a pointed nail to pull the bandages away from his skin. The smell of his blood instantly hit her nose as soon as the bandages were off. She tensed at the sight of the red liquid.

"I can do it myself if the sight of blood scares you," he offered, surprised by her sudden fear of blood despite being a healer.

She shook her head. "I will be fine. This paste may sting a bit." She dipped her fingers into the paste and began to gently rub it onto the wound in his shoulder.

Adair hissed and dug his fingers into the blankets on the cot when he felt an awful, burning sting run through his wound and ripple throughout his body. Halona's hands began to glow as she used her magic to heal a small part of the wound. The pain in his shoulder intensified and he let out a string of curses. "That is more than a *bit* of stinging." He seethed.

Halona's lips curled into an amused smirk, but she stayed focused as she worked on healing the stubborn man.

"You were hit in the shoulder and the upper part of your chest," she explained as she pulled her hands away.

The pain in Adair's body faded to a dull ache after she cut off the magic. Halona slowly began to bandage the wounds.

"Because healing magic is painful for the person being healed, healers don't use much of it. If I use a little bit every day, it will help build your tendons and muscle back to normal." She finished with the last bandage and stepped back to admire her handiwork.

She caught herself staring at the man's chest longer than was proper. Her face flushed a light pink and she turned around to organize something in the cabinets.

Adair rolled his eyes at the strange girl's actions. He carefully laid back down on the cot to get some rest. As he closed his eyes, he prayed that he would not have to relive Bennett's death again.

Chapter 7

Adair felt like he was floating. He slowly opened his eyes to see that he was hovering in midair. There was nothing but darkness surrounding him. He suddenly began to feel as if he were falling fast. He hit the ground with a thud. Panicking, he began to look around. He ran forward, looking around suspiciously. Slowly, the darkness began to lighten. Things began to blur together before the image of a forest surrounded him. He soon realized that he was no longer running. He was riding on the back of his horse.

Still uneasy and confused, he continued to glance around. His men were riding alongside him. They were all laughing and smiling. He even saw Bennett's smiling face.

Slowly, Adair's fear began to melt away. His men were alive. He reached out to grasp Bennett's shoulder, but the man slapped his hand away. The smile on Bennett's face turned into a scowl.

"You let me die, Adair," Bennett spoke with a deep, dark tone. "You ran while I was killed. You left me to die. You could have saved me, and now my child will be fatherless."

Adair's eyes widened and he looked around at the rest of the men. They all looked at him with the same hatred in their eyes.

"You let us die," the men began to chant. Blood began to run down their faces from their eyes. "You let us die, so you must die."

The men pointed their weapons at the prince. "You must die." They continued to chant.

Adair firmly grasped the reins of his horse and kicked at its sides. The horse bolted away from the angry mob. Adair panted and never looked back, but what he saw in front of him frightened him even more.

44

The men that he had just left were standing there, right in front of him. They were still chanting. Each one began to turn around. Their eyes were replaced with black holes, blood still dripping from the sockets.

"You let us die. You must die." They continued chanting as they slowly walked toward the prince.

Adair made a quick turn to run away. When he thought he was far enough away, the men appeared again. The chanting grew louder as they got closer. Adair felt a sharp pain in his shoulder. He turned and saw Bennett smirking. Blood dripped from the man's mouth. Bennett's sword pierced Adair's left shoulder. A scream erupted from the prince as everything went black once more.

Chapter 8

Halona jolted awake when she heard the scream. She had fallen asleep at the desk in the medical hut to stay near Adair and keep an eye on him. The scream had scared her enough to knock her out of her chair, causing her shoulder to hit the corner desk. She hissed in pain before grabbing onto the desk with her other arm.

Once she was on her feet, she walked to Adair's side. He was thrashing around in his sleep. His stitches had come out, causing his wound to reopen. Blood was seeping through the bandages and dripping onto the cot.

"Adair," she called out as she tried to calm him.

He continued to thrash. His body was much larger than hers and she was unable to restrain him. His thrashing caused him to knock her to the ground. She hissed again as her injured side bumped the cot.

She got back onto her feet and tried to stop his squirming once again. "Adair, calm down," she whispered. The writhing did not stop. Mariana, startled by the commotion, rushed from the back room into the front of the hut.

"What is happening?" she asked and ran to Adair's bedside to help the small girl restrain him.

Halona shook her head and gripped her injured side. Mariana was larger than Halona and that made it easier for her to hold the prince's body down.

"You take care of your side, dear. I'll take care of him." Mariana gave the girl a worried glance.

Halona nodded and took her hand from her side. Blood started to seep through her clothes as her stitches came open. She removed her vest and pulled her shirt over her head before unwrapping her bandages. She tugged the old stitches out of her skin while biting down on her lower lip to silence a cry. Her shaky hands held up the needle and thread. She slowly began to sew her wound closed. It was not a clean stitch, but it would have to do. She dipped her fingers into a bowl of paste. After inhaling a deep breath, she gently massaged the paste into her skin and over the wound. She hissed in pain and bit down on her lip harder. Once the stitches and wound were covered with paste, she placed her hand over the area. Her hand began to faintly glow as her magic worked. When she finished, she flopped into the chair at the desk and began to clean the blood from the rest of her abdomen before she pulled her shirt back on.

While Halona was bandaging herself, Mariana tried to restrain Adair to stop his thrashing. She could not do it on her own. Luckily, Evan heard the commotion as he walked by on his way to train with Severin. He stopped inside to check on things and Mariana requested his help. Together, the two of them restrained Adair with rope, hindering his thrashing.

"Damn," Evian heaved. Restraining the prince had been a struggle for both him and Mariana. They were both panting.

Adair awoke breathing heavily and covered in sweat. He frowned at the ropes once he realized he had been tied to the bed.

Halona walked to Adair's bedside. "Are you all right?" she asked as she placed a wet cloth to his forehead. Adair's eyes were still darting around nervously. Mariana slowly began to clean and stitch his wound before covering it with bandages. He groaned in pain and tried to squirm out of the rope ties.

"Adair, stop. Mariana is trying to close your shoulder wound. Your stitches came out." Halona spoke in a soothing voice to calm him while Mariana worked to cover his wound.

His eyes continued to dart around as he cringed from the pain. "I shouldn't be alive," he whimpered. "I should have died with the others."

Halona sighed and sat in the chair beside his cot. "Adair, you are alive for a reason. You are a Peace Bringer. You have to live."

His blue eyes narrowed at her. "Boarshit. I am tired of hearing about this damn prophecy. Fate does not exist! Either kill me, or let me go."

"Adair, you know that I can't do that," Halona said. She frowned as she crossed her arms.

Adair knew she was right, but he would never admit it.

"My father will eventually learn that I am missing and my men are dead. When he does, he will send an army. He will slaughter every single one of you filthy savages," he spat.

It was Halona's turn to narrow her eyes. She wrapped a hand around his throat and growled. The tips of her sharp nails dug into his flesh. "Listen here, you ungrateful bastard. You and I are Peace Bringers, but my father is the Avory's leader and he has a clan to protect. If your father's men so much as step inside our borders with the intent to harm my people, they will be slaughtered just like your friends, and I will make sure that you witness all of it."

Halona let go of Adair's throat and took Evian by the arm, dragging him from the hut.

"Where are we going?" Evian asked. He looked from his sister to the hut.

"To Severin. I want to train."

"Absolutely not. You are injured. We are not going to fight you," Evian scolded, always protective of his sister.

Her eyes rolled and she continued dragging her brother along behind her. Evian protested the entire way to the training grounds, just on the outskirts of the village in a large field. There were plenty of targets for archery practice and plenty of practice mannequins for attacking. The siblings reached the area in about ten minutes. Severin was already training, hacking and kicking away at a mannequin.

"Yo, Severin," Evian called out as they approached.

Severin stopped mid-kick and turned to wave at his younger siblings. "Halona, what are you doing here?"

"I want to train," she stated. Severin shook his head and glared at Evian as he approached.

Evian waved his hands in the air frantically. "Hey, I told her no. Besides, she didn't even bring her bow."

"I can always go get it," she offered.

"Absolutely not," Severin spoke, walking toward them. He stood with his arms crossed in front of Halona. She opened her mouth to protest, but Severin cut her off. "You are not training today. Your wound is not healed. I will not risk it."

She opened her mouth to speak once more, but Severin knew what she was thinking before she could speak. "Halona, Evian does not have a serious injury like you do."

Halona huffed and sat down in the grass. Severin had put his foot down and there was no way she would be able to change his mind. She grumbled to herself as she watched her two brothers prepare to spar with one another.

Severin's longsword was firmly grasped in his hands. Evian's grip was weak and flimsy. She quietly listened as Severin instructed his younger brother to tighten his grip.

"No, no. That's too tight," Severin groaned. "You don't want your knuckles turning purple."

Evian loosened his grip again, but too much. Severin easily knocked the sword out of his hands. The sword flew and Severin snatched it from its flightpath. Evian frowned as his older brother tossed the sword back to him. The two readied themselves again. It only took a few seconds for Severin to steal Evian's sword once more.

Becoming frustrated, Evian's swings and thrusts became frantic. He paid no attention to his surroundings as he swung madly. Severin's face remained void of emotion while he easily deflected Evian's poor attacks.

"Don't let your emotions get the better of you," Severin instructed. "Keep a level head."

Halona's mind began to wander as she grew tired. Slowly, she slipped into a light sleep. Her soft breathing was silent compared to the sound of clashing metal from her brothers' blades.

Severin caught the sleeping form of his sister from the corner of his eye just as he had taken Evian's sword from him for a seventh time. He stopped his fight with Evian by dropping both swords and raising a hand to his chest as a sign of surrender.

Evian, puzzled by his brother's reaction to his poor fighting skills, cocked his head to the side. Severin's only response was to point to their sister's peaceful form as she slept on the grass of the practice field.

Evian let out a soft chuckle. "We'd better get her home."

Severin nodded before carefully bringing his sister into his arms. He was careful not to touch her injury. She subconsciously curled into his chest with a smile as the pair took her back home.

Chapter 9

King Roland sat at the head of the table. Around him, sat his advisors. Normally, Adair would be on his left, but it had been five days and the boy had not returned. Queen Abry was becoming increasingly paranoid and they both were losing sleep over it. King Roland was concerned, but he wanted to believe that his son was only taking his time to find the perfect trophy. Adair never did anything half-way. He was always a "go big or go home" type of man.

"Your Highness."

King Roland was startled out of his thoughts. He cleared his throat and looked to see Eyra, Aria's prophet.

"Yes, Eyra," the king said, glancing at his advisor.

"I have had another vision," Eyra said. "Conflict will begin soon on our borders between Uron and Etras. This will be the beginning of the Great War mentioned at the prince's birth."

The king nodded as he tried to listen to his advisors. Each one had a different matter to discuss. One mentioned the numbers of professional soldiers in the Arian army verses the number of citizens that would need to be drafted which, of course, would cause worry among the Arian people.

His thoughts kept returning to his son. Where was Adair? He had to be alive, or Eyra would have known of his death. Why had he not returned yet? The grounds of the Royal Hunt were miles from any savage border. Adair would return soon; King Roland had a gut feeling. When Adair returned, there would be a feast. In the meantime, Roland needed to ready his army for war.

◇•◇•◇

Chapter 10

dair groaned as he tried to make sense of the Avory language in one of the books that Halona had left for him. He put his bookmark back on the page and dropped the book to the floor beside the bed. While he was busy reading, Mariana had made him another cup of herbs to drink. He knew he needed it because he could feel the ache returning to his muscles.

He picked up the cup and quickly gulped the liquid. Mariana had made the herb drink more tolerable. He did not know what she added to it, but it made his throat burn less, and the drink had a sweeter taste. He sighed as he finished the drink. He was becoming too accustomed to this. He wondered if his father had sent men to come looking for him yet. He let out another sigh just as Halona entered the hut.

"What's gotten into you?" she asked.

"It's none of your business."

Halona shrugged as she set about her routine of cleaning, organizing, and stocking the medical hut. As she was doing so, two men came in carrying an injured man. His leg was sliced open and dripping blood as they set him on an empty cot.

"What happened?" Halona asked as she began to gather her supplies. She flinched at the sight of the blood.

"He cut himself chopping wood," one man said.

She set about cleaning and bandaging his wound as she used her magic to heal it.

"Be more careful from now on," she instructed when she finished dressing the wound. "Take it easy for the rest of the day and come back tomorrow. I will look at it then to see if I need to do anything more."

The man bowed to her. "Thank you, Princess. You really are a gift from the Moon."

Halona thanked him and sent him on his way with instructions to be careful.

Once the men were gone, Adair scoffed. "Gift my ass. You haven't been able to heal me fully yet."

Halona ignored him as she began to clean the blood off the floor of the hut. While she worked, Adair continued to spout nonsense and vulgarities about the prophecy. She clenched her teeth and continued to ignore him.

"I mean, you worship the moon. How stupid is that? The moon is a giant rock in the sky. There is nothing special about it."

Seething, Halona turned around and came unglued. She pointed a finger into Adair's face and began to shout.

"Keep your mouth shut about our goddess. I haven't said anything bad about your people the entire time you have been here, yet you continue to belittle and degrade my people and our beliefs."

Adair opened his mouth to speak, but Halona cut him off.

"I don't want to hear it," she said as she stormed out of the hut.

Mariana stood outside the door and called after Halona, but the girl did not stop. Before Halona knew it, she had left the village and began to head toward the small lake outside of town.

Halona never had doubts about her faith in the prophecies. Her mother had been the daughter of a prophet from another clan, but never received the Sight that gave the prophets their visions. Whenever Adair disrespected the prophecies and the prophets, Halona felt as if he was offending her ancestry.

She sat at the bank and cried for some time before deciding to return to the medical hut. When she walked in, Mariana was there tending to Adair's wound. The rest of the mess from before the argument was cleaned.

Halona and Adair briefly made eye contact, but quickly averted their gazes. It was childish and they both knew it, but neither cared.

"You two can't hate each other forever," Mariana lightly teased, trying to calm them both down. "As Peace Bringers, you will have to work together to save Salacir. You can't do that if you're at each other's throats."

Adair scoffed, but did not say a word as Halona began to forcefully peal the bandages away from his skin. She smirked when Adair cried out from the pain.

"It seems you're healing faster than we thought," Mariana said as she inspected Adair's wound. "We might be able to use a little more magic than normal to seal the rest of your wound up."

Adair's ears perked. He could be healed today? Wonderful, he thought. He could sneak away and head home first chance he got.

Halona frowned at the prince's hopeful expression. "That doesn't mean you can leave. You're still stuck here. Everyone will be on guard even more with an Arian man running around. You'll be killed the first time you try to escape."

"Says who?" Adair responded childishly.

"Says me," a deep voice rang from the door of the hut. The trio's heads turned. Roka was standing in the doorway with his arms crossed. He had a sword sheathed at his hip. He was covered in scratches and a few slices.

"Sir, what happened to you?" Mariana's eyes widened as she began to gather herbs to fix the small wounds on her leader's arms.

Roka shrugged and shooed the woman away. "I will be fine, Mariana. I had some time off, so I went to the training grounds to spar with Severin."

Mariana let out a sigh of relief, but then frowned. "That boy is too skilled for his own good."

Roka let out a deep laugh and placed a warm hand on the woman's shoulder. "Relax. I expect nothing less from my sons."

Halona turned away from the two and looked at Adair. His eyebrow was raised. Mariana and Roka continued to talk to one another and eventually left the two young adults alone.

"What is the matter with you?" Adair laughed. The girl was frowning with her head hung low. Her red hair fell in front of her eyes.

"Nothing," she whispered, before standing and grabbing the supplies that Mariana left on the counter. Adair gave her a puzzled look. Halona seemed upset suddenly, and it bothered him, but he could not explain why. He had never been bothered by a girl's emotions before.

"You don't have to talk to me about it because I honestly don't care, but if you need to get something off your chest, go right ahead," he said.

Halona shook her head as she began to clean his wound with a wet cloth. "I'm fine," she said, her voice cracking. Adair did not push further. If the stupid girl did not want to talk, then she did not want to talk.

Halona grabbed a paste that she had made earlier. It was different than the one she used when she used her magic. It was a cream color and smelled like a riverbank. "How are you doing?" she whispered quietly as she rubbed the paste into his wound. "Since your men . . . you know."

She could not bring herself to say the word, but Adair knew what she meant. Without thinking, he responded.

"It's only been ten days. I'm coping, if you can call it that. I'm having nightmares, so I try not to sleep more than I should. I'm eating enough to keep me alive. All I really want to do is go home. My mother is probably worried sick."

She nodded. "I can try to help with the nightmares if you want me too. My mother used to sing me a lullaby whenever I would have bad dreams as a child."

Adair frowned. "I'm not a child and I don't need your pity."

Halona shook her head and chuckled softly. Adair watched as Halona's hands began to glow. The color was much brighter than all the other times before, causing the room to light up in multiple shades of green. The pain was also worse. Adair hissed and gripped the sheets on the cot as her magic continued to heal him.

When she finished, they were both panting. She had used too much energy, and he had been in too much pain. She dropped into the chair to catch her breath while he laid there waiting for the pain to disappear.

When it finally did, he looked down at his shoulder. The wound was completely healed. He grinned and brought his arm up high into the air. He twisted it around a few times to loosen the muscles and the joint.

Adair looked at Halona sitting in the chair, still panting and gasping for air. It had taken much more magic and energy than she had thought. Blood was seeping through her bandages from the stress she put her body under while trying to heal him. Adair knew this was his chance to escape. This was his chance to go home. He could run now while Halona was recovering and while Roka was preoccupied with Mariana.

Adair stood and stared at the door. He took two wobbly steps, but stopped, a strong force holding him in place. His mind was telling him to run. It was telling him to go home to his parents and his people, but his body would not move. He glanced toward Halona. She was still gasping and coughing, completely oblivious to him. His body started to move, but not toward the door. He began moving toward her. He knelt at her side as she gasped and shook. He placed a tan hand on her pale arm. A jolt of electricity shot through them both and the diamond on his forehead began to glow. They both sat there staring at one another in shock and amazement as the soft green light shone between them. Halona's breathing slowed and the glow faded. Adair stared at his hands, confused.

"You really are a Peace Bringer," Halona said.

"Boarshit," he answered, still looking down at his hands. "How did I do that?"

"Peace Bringers have a bond that allows them to share energy. I've only heard about it in the stories. I've never seen it in person. I needed help and, just by touching my arm, you gave it."

Adair blinked, still confused. Halona laughed at his confusion and patted his head. "You have a lot to learn."

Chapter 11

"It's been two weeks, Roland. Something is wrong!" Queen Abry paced the floor of her bedroom. Her hair was a mess, and her eyes were red and puffy from crying. King Roland sat on the bed with his head in his hands. He had spent so much time ignoring his wife's superstitions, but he was beginning to think it was possible that she was right. Their son could be dead.

King Roland stood and headed for the door. Queen Abry repeatedly asked where he was headed, but he did not respond. He kept walking until he found himself at Eyra's quarters. If anyone knew if the prince was still alive, it would be the old advisor. The king knocked loudly. It took several moments before the door finally slid open. Eyra did not look surprised to see the king.

"Your Majesty," he said, and bowed.

King Roland rushed into the room. "Eyra, I must know for my wife's sake. Is our son alive?"

"Yes, Your Majesty. Adair is alive. He is well and in good hands," Eyra spoke softly. The wise old man walked to a bookcase on the other side of the wall.

"Whose hands? He has not returned from his hunt. No one from that trip has returned. I need to know if anything has happened," the King spoke insistently. Eyra pulled a small scroll from the shelf and unraveled it.

"Something, indeed, did happen, but I assure you that our Prince Adair is safe. Alas, he will not be able to return to us for some time. He has met the other child of the prophecy," Eyra said. The old man's eyes scanned the scroll before he rolled it back up and returned it to the shelf.

"What happened, Eyra? Tell me," the king ordered.

Eyra glanced at his king and nodded.

"As you wish, Your Majesty," he began. "The hunting party found themselves trapped in savage lands. Our dear prince is the sole survivor of a savage attack. He is now in the savage village living alongside them as a prisoner. He is safe. They will not harm him because he is a Peace Bringer. You have nothing to fear."

King Roland fumed. Those filthy heathens had not attacked anyone in his land in years, and now those demons were holding his son prisoner?

"Before you do anything rash, Your Majesty, remember that Adair is meant to end this war after months of bloodshed. In order to do that, he must be with the savage girl who is meant to help him. It would be pointless to send an army after him when the army would be better off heading into the battlefield. The Uronian army will be advancing toward our border any day now," Eyra said, trying to reason with the king. The old man knew there were two ways that this could go. The king would agree to let Adair carry out his destiny in the savage lands, or the king would send an army to try to retrieve his only son.

The king said nothing as he stormed out of the seer's quarters.

Chapter 12

"Must we do this?" Adair grumbled. Halona nodded and opened the book in her lap.

Adair had been in the Avory village for weeks and he was still staying in the medical hut. He was beginning to come to terms with having to stay in the village. Since the day he had used magic to help Halona, he was slowly beginning to understand the prophecy. Halona had been helpful, as well. She was constantly trying to teach him how life in her village worked or what was expected of them as Peace Bringers.

"Who is the Moon Spirit?" Halona quizzed the prince. He shook his head. He knew the answer.

"Your god," he stated confidently.

Halona smiled. "Yes, the Moon Spirit is like a god to us. She watches over our lands. The legend is that she was once a beautiful woman with white hair and eyes as dark as the night sky. She fell in love with a man named Polaris, but she could not be with him because they were from rival clans. Every night they would sneak out to see one another and she would dance for him. Then one day, she and Polaris created the magic we use for healing. The two managed to combine their energy into a large enough force that they could ascend to the sky to be together for all eternity. The Moon Spirit was so happy that she began to dance around the Earth with her love. Every night, the two lovers' energy lights up the night sky as the Moon and the North Star."

Adair yawned. "Boring."

Halona frowned and elbowed him in the ribcage. "Don't call our Mistress Moon boring! It's a romantic story!"

Adair raised his hands in defense. "I'm just not fond of romance."

Halona rolled her eyes and elbowed him again. "I didn't expect you to be."

"Stop doing that!" Adair frowned as he rubbed his side. He continued to frown at the girl, but all she did was laugh at him. Eventually, he found himself laughing along with her.

"Next lesson," she said with a smile and opened another book to the map Adair had been studying.

"This map has every clan in Salacir listed." She pointed to the borders of Aria and then to a small patch in the west. "This is the Avory clan lands."

Adair rolled his eyes. He already knew where to find the Avory lands and Aria on a map. What he was most curious about were the little triangles that seemed to mark paths through all the countries.

"What are those triangles for?" He pointed to one drawn on the map in the western region of Etras.

Halona frowned. "The triangles mean the clan is nomadic. The one you are pointing to is the Mercants. They tend to specialize in trade more often than combat. It's about the time of year when they come through this area to trade with us."

She pointed to another triangle near Aria's eastern border, "This is the Itis. Their customs are probably what your people think of when they think of any of the clans."

Adair raised his eyebrow. He pointed to the bone necklace around her neck, "You have human bones around your neck. Those signify that you are a savage."

Halona frowned. "These are rabbit bones," she stated matter-of-factly. "I'm not a psycho."

Adair's eyes narrowed. "You have human heads surrounding the borders of your clan's territory. That is one of the biggest signs that one has found savage land. What about those? That's how my men and I knew we were on your lands." His eyes dimmed for a minute as he remembered those moments before the massacre started.

Halona snorted before she began laughing hysterically. She spat out words between laughs. "Those weren't heads!"

Adair frowned and opened his mouth to speak, but Halona cut him off. "It's a tactic we use to keep people away from our lands. Because we have not seen battle in years, we do not have real heads to place on the spikes. Those 'heads' you saw were decaying fruit painted to look like human faces. Believe it or not, the Avory are very artistic."

Adair's jaw dropped. The head that had terrified him so much was a fruit? He sat there with his mouth open for several moments. Halona laughed harder. Before long, Adair found himself laughing along with her.

Evian entered the hut and stared at the duo strangely. He cleared his throat, causing the two to look over at him.

"Yes?" Halona snickered as she batted her eyelashes at her brother. Evian shook his head with a chuckle.

"Pops wanted me to tell you that Adair is going to start sleeping in our house," he said. Turning his head in Adair's direction, he continued, "That doesn't mean our father trusts you."

Halona nodded and glanced at Adair. "Better pack your things," she teased. Since he had been healed, Roka and Mariana had hidden his weapons and armor, much to the prince's chagrin.

Groaning, Adair stood straight up. Now that he was standing, he noticed that he was a great deal taller than Halona. She barely reached his torso. Adair saw the frown on her face. He smirked and gave her head a soft pat in silent mocking.

"Moron," she mumbled with a frown as she turned to follow Evian home.

"You really should expand your vocabulary, Halona," Evian teased as he ruffled his sister's hair.

Halona stomped on his foot. "Shut up, Moron!"

Adair chuckled to himself and followed the siblings to their home. He glanced around the village as they walked. This was his first time out of the medical hut. He was astonished at how the buildings were constructed. They were not much different from the buildings he saw in the capital.

"How many people live in your village?" he asked curiously.

Halona tapped her chin in concentration as she thought. "Well, the last time Father had a census collected, there were two-hundred-sixty people in the clan. That was in the fall. We've had dozens of babies born since then, so I would say that the total numbers are probably close to three-hundred."

When they entered Roka's large house, Adair looked around, surprised. He knew Roka's house would not be as extravagant as Adair's palace, but compared to the small size of all the other houses, the place was gigantic.

He noticed Halona's other two brothers sitting in a couple of the chairs. He did not recognize them, but assumed they were her family. The red hair, pale skin, and freckled faces were unmistakable, and no one else that he had seen had that appearance. He turned his head to the kitchen where a delicious aroma filled his senses.

Mariana exited from the kitchen area to inform everyone that dinner was ready.

"Mariana's cooking is the best," Halona said.

Evian nodded and addressed his sister. "It's much better than your cooking. Last time you cooked, you nearly poisoned us."

"Moron!" Halona shouted as she threw her shoe at her brother's head. It barely missed and landed across the room.

Adair awkwardly sat in another chair. He noticed Severin, another of Halona's brothers, staring at him. Adair felt as if the man's emerald eyes were seeing directly into his soul. He cleared his throat and gave the man a threatening glance. The two sat there glaring at one another for several minutes as the others carried on conversation. The staring contest ended when Liam came up behind his brother.

"Severin, stop trying to scare the poor boy," Liam laughed as he leaned over his twin's shoulder.

Adair's lips drew into a smirk as Severin's green eyes moved to Liam.

Halona and Mariana shared glances with one another. Both saw the thick tension between Adair and Severin.

"Well, why don't we eat?" Mariana smiled.

Chapter 13

"Your Majesty, this is not the way to solve this problem. I assure you, Prince Adair is safe." Eyra stood in front of the livid King of Aria's desk. King Roland had given the orders to his general to begin assembling a small army to retrieve Adair from the clutches of the vile savages.

"I've made up my mind, Eyra. This is my decision. Adair has been gone for two weeks. I will not stand by while my son is in the hands of savages," King Roland said. The man stood, clearly finished listening. The Queen had become distraught and ill with grief and King Roland could not bear to see her suffer any longer.

The king looked menacing to the old seer.

"Sire, this will only end badly. I have seen what will happen no matter your decision," the old man began to explain. "It is safer for Adair to stay where he is. You will lose many men if you send that army."

King Roland refused to listen. He was sending men after his son. Their orders were to kill every savage they came across. There would be no mercy. The Avory would burn.

Eyra opened his mouth to speak again. He never got his chance because a knock sounded on the heavy wooden door.

General Thomas entered and bowed to his king. "Sir, the men are ready to leave at your command."

King Roland returned to his chair. He placed his hands under his chin. "Go. Bring my son back." He glanced at Eyra and pointed. "And throw that man into a cell. I want him tried for treason."

"Sir!" Eyra stood, flabbergasted. He had not expected this, but then again, he never saw visions of his own fate, only those of the people around him.

General Thomas bowed and left the room. It did not take long for two guards to return and drag Eyra from the room. He continued to shout to the king about his mistake until he was in the dark, damp depths of the prison.

As General Thomas and his men left the capital gates, dark storm clouds began rolling across the sky. The distant sound of thunder could be heard, but none of the men paid attention. Their goal was to find Prince Adair. A silly storm was not going to get in their way.

Chapter 14

The sky turned black as the storm clouds rolled in over the Avory village. Halona and Adair looked up from their spot on the training field. Evian and Severin were training with their swords. Evian, as usual, was losing. His arm was bloody with scrapes and cuts. Halona's older brothers were deeply engrossed in their sparring match and neither noticed the dark clouds filling the sky.

"We should go inside," Halona shouted to her brothers as she rose to her feet. The wind was picking up speed and slowly beginning to howl. Severin and Evian stopped their fight to look at their sister and then to the sky.

"Looks like this is going to be a rough one," Severin said before he sheathed his sword and walked to the pair in the grass. Evian grumbled that a little rain was not going to hurt them. Suddenly, a huge flash of lightning filled the sky. It was followed by a clash of thunder. Evian stopped his protesting and sheathed his sword.

"Let's go," he muttered as he quickly walked past his siblings and Adair. The prince frowned as he looked up at the sky. Droplets of water began to fall. Storms this bad were a rare occurrence in the center of Aria, but he had experienced enough to know they could be terrible. The last devastating storm had occurred when Adair was fourteen.

Adair stood in his father's study as the king looked over paperwork. It had been three days since the storm tore through the heart of Aria. There had

been minimal damage to the palace, but the capital and surrounding villages had been left in shambles.

"Another forty bodies were found in Salvin," King Roland said. He sighed as he ran a hand through his dark beard. He passed the paperwork to young Adair.

"Son, what would you do in a situation like this? You have people without homes and food. There were entire villages wiped out in this storm. If you were king, how would you respond?"

Adair looked to his father and then back at the papers in his hands. "I would send men into the damaged areas to clear debris and search for survivors."

King Roland nodded. "That's all well and good, but what do you do when you find these survivors?"

Adair did not need to think long before he answered. "I would supply them with food and the materials needed to rebuild their homes and villages."

King Roland nodded once more. "You're on your way to becoming a good king, Adair, but you must remember one important thing. In order to help your people, you need money for their food and supplies. What happens if the country's economy is struggling?"

Adair searched and searched for an answer, but he could not come up with one. Disappointed, he stayed quiet through the rest of the meeting. He watched and listened as his father gave his advisors and generals orders. Adair could not help but think that he would never be as great a king as his father.

"Adair!" The shout broke the young man from his thoughts. He turned toward the sound and noticed that the others were leaving him behind. His hair was already soaked by the falling rain.

"Come on!" Halona shouted.

Adair raced to catch up with the three siblings. The wind shook the trees around them and lightning flashed through the sky. Thunder roared above them as the group ran back to the safety of Roka's house.

They were close when Adair heard faint meowing. He searched and eventually saw a small, orange kitten shivering. The poor creature was soaked to the bone and trapped in a barrel. More meowing could be heard a grey kitten came into view. The barrel was quickly filling with water and the kittens would drown if he did not do something. Without a second thought, Adair reached in and pulled the two baby cats from the barrel. He held them close to his chest and tugged his cloak closed before running forward to catch up with the others.

"What took you so long?" Halona shouted as Adair reached the door to the house. He said nothing as the wind howled around them. The two quickly rushed into the dry home.

Roka, who had been standing by the door waiting on the two to come inside, shut the door and barricaded it. His eyebrows furrowed when he heard meows coming from Adair's chest. He looked down and smirked at the sight of the two kittens in the prince's arms. He said nothing as he walked away.

Halona scooped the grey kitten into her own hands. "They're adorable!"

Liam, who had already been in the house at the start of the storm, scratched a kitten behind its ear. "Where'd you find them?"

Adair laughed as the orange kitten clutched onto his shirt with its claws. "They were in a barrel. The rain was causing it to fill with water and they were going to drown."

"I knew there was a heart beating in that chest of yours!" Evian gushed, and poked Adair in the forehead.

The younger man frowned and swatted at Evian's hand. Halona disappeared during the boys' tussle and returned with a couple of small towels. She set her kitten down on the towel and began to dry the little creature. It meowed and squirmed. Once she was finished, she traded kittens with Adair and began drying the other one.

Roka returned to the room with a saucer. He set it on the floor in front of the fire and watched as the two kittens ran to it to begin lapping up the warm milk.

Halona sat beside the kittens and ran her fingers through their soft fur. When it was finished drinking from the saucer, one kitten meowed before crawling into her lap. It purred and slowly fell asleep.

Everyone huddled around the fire to stay warm. The wind continued to howl outside. The house shook against the force of the storm and the sound of rain pounding on the roof filled the house. A bright flash of lightning lit up the dark sky outside. The flash was immediately followed by a loud crash of thunder.

The kittens jolted at the sound and their terrified mews filled the room. Mariana stood and exited, returning with a small basket. She placed a towel inside before setting both kittens within it. They continued to meow, but eventually the wind and thunder drowned out their complaints.

Halona pulled her knees to her chest. With every roar of thunder, she twitched. Evian sat beside her with her head resting on his shoulders. Every time she twitched, he would stroke her hair.

Adair watched the family curiously. They seemed so close to one another. It reminded him of his parents. He stood and moved to one of the empty chairs. He leaned his head back and closed his eyes. Silently, he wondered what his life would have been like if he had grown up with siblings.

Ignoring everyone he passed, Adair ran as fast as his legs could carry him. He needed to get to his mother. He threw open the door to his parents' room.

"Mother!" He shouted as he rushed to her side. She was ill and lying in bed. King Roland was on her left, and the Royal Doctor was on her right. Queen Abry smiled at her son and took his hand.

"I'm fine, Adair," the woman said and smiled at her thirteen-year-old son. While she appeared happy, Adair knew better. Her face was red and splotchy as if she had been crying. His father's grim expression was no comfort.

"Then what is wrong?" Adair frowned.

"Your baby sister," answered King Roland. He spoke with a gruff voice. His speech wavered as he tried to coax the words from his mouth. "She did not survive."

Queen Abry's smile faded. Adair watched as his mother's smiling face was once again filled with tears. He looked between his parents. That was when he finally noticed the small bundle in his mother's arms. He leaned over and peaked at the tiny body within the pink blanket. There was no sign of life in her little body.

Queen Abry clutched the baby to her chest as she sobbed. King Roland grasped her hand in his. Adair stood over his parents with worry etched all over his young face. His mother had been so delighted to have another child. That happiness had been replaced with so much sorrow. It had only been a matter of hours. Adair could not bear it any longer. He kissed his mother's head and quickly left the room. He vowed that he would never see his mother cry like that again. He would make sure that she was always smiling.

◇•◇•◇

nother clash of thunder brought Adair from his thoughts. The fire glowed. It lit the room in a dull orange glow. The kittens were still meowing, and the wind was still howling. Rain continued to pound on the roof of the hut.

Nothing had changed except for Halona. She was shivering more than the kittens had been earlier. She was pressed into Evian's chest as he tried to calm her down. Every clap of thunder made her shivering worse. Her whimper rivaled the meows.

Mariana disappeared once more before reappearing with an arm full of blankets. She passed them out to everyone. Adair thanked her when she handed him one. He wrapped it around himself and leaned his head into the soft fabric of the chair.

Roka stood by the window checking the weather and conditions of the village.

"You should all get some rest," he said, and looked around at his children, Mariana, and Adair. "This storm won't be letting up anytime soon."

Evian nodded to his father before standing with his sister in his arms. He walked to one of the bigger chairs and sat in it. Halona curled herself into his chest as he wrapped a blanket around the two of them. She continued to shake and shiver until she fell asleep.

Adair closed his eyes as he drifted into a light sleep. Everyone slowly wandered into their own dreams.

Chapter 15

dair stood at the front of Roka's home with the kittens in his arms. Roka was assessing the damage done by the storm the night before. Some of the buildings were heavily damaged, but for the most part, the village was still standing. He could not help but mentally applaud the way the buildings had been designed to withstand windstorms. Liam and Roka began doing rounds of the village to make sure everyone was safe. Others were scurrying to fix the damaged homes.

Halona appeared at Adair's side. He gave her a sideways glance. Her hair was sticking up in various places. Her eyes and face were red. She had not slept well the night before.

"Stop staring at me, Moron," she grumbled as she glared at him.

"I would never stare at your ugly mug." Adair rolled his eyes.

Halona scoffed. "I know that I look terrible. You don't have to rub it in."

Annoyed with the prince, Halona walked along the limb-covered path to get to the medical hut. Adair followed with the basket of kittens still in his arms.

When they arrived, Mariana was already there standing on the outside of what should have been the medial hut, but instead was a pile of rubble. She sighed and shook her head before beginning to rummage through the pile. Halona kneeled to help the woman.

"Princess, that isn't necessary," Mariana scolded.

Halona scoffed again, "Yes, it is. I want to help."

Mariana let out another sigh. "Alright," she spoke as she dug a quill and paper from her pocket. "Go get me these herbs from the area around Lake Almond. Our supply was destroyed in the storm."

She handed the paper and a basket to Halona before heading to talk to someone about repairing the hut.

Halona glanced over the list before turning on her heels and walking down a path that led out of the village. Adair looked around for a place to leave the kittens and finally settled on leaving them in front of the destroyed hut. He quickly caught up with Halona.

They walked along for several minutes in silence. Halona gave the basket to Adair while she braided her hair as they walked. Adair looked around, noticing that the area seemed familiar. He was about to ask about it when he saw the mounds of dirt. Each one had a stone and a weapon sticking up from the top. He stared at them and counted them one by one.

"Father sent several men out after your party was attacked to bury your comrades," Halona spoke softly as she glanced at Adair from the corner of her eye.

Adair stopped in his tracks and stared at each of the piles. Images from that night flashed through his mind, followed by the images from the nightmares he had been experiencing. He walked alongside each of the graves, mumbling under his breath.

"I'm sorry," he said over and over. He stopped at a familiar blade. Adair fell to his knees at the grave of his best friend. He recognized black hilt wrapped in silver beads. Adair had given him the beads as a wedding present only a year ago. His friend's family crest was on the side of the hilt and the Arian Crest was at the bottom. Tears began streaming down Adair's cheeks as he reached out to touch the weapon.

"I'm sorry, Bennett," he choked out the words as he grabbed the hilt of the sword. He began to pull it from the ground.

"Woah!" Halona frowned, rushing to Adair's side. She gripped the sword and pushed it back into the dirt before it could be removed any further. "You can't pull that from the ground!"

Adair raised his head enough to stare at the girl. He was about to ask why he should not touch the sword, but she spoke.

"It's considered disrespectful to the dead. By taking the weapon from the grave, you are robbing it and desecrating the deceased's memory." Her eyes were frantic as they darted between the sword and Adair.

Adair looked down at the blade. Part of his mind was telling him to ignore the girl and take the sword. In Aria, blades were always given to someone else when the original owner died. Another part of his mind was telling him to leave it. He struggled inwardly for several minutes before deciding the sword was better off in the dirt. Roka would probably confiscate it anyway.

Halona let out a sigh of relief and bowed her head as she kneeled in the dirt. She placed her hand on the pile and muttered words in a language that Adair did not understand. When she finished, she stood and motioned for him to follow. "Come on."

Adair nodded and stood. His face was stained with tears. Halona turned around and handed him a green handkerchief. He blinked and took it from her. He dabbed his eyes with it before handing it back. She slipped it back into her pocket and continued to walk down the path.

"It should be another ten minutes and we'll be at Lake Almond," she said, fidgeting with her braid.

Adair sensed the girl's discomfort. "Do you not like this place?"

Halona stopped and turned to look back at him. "I love it. It's just that I have too many fond memories of being at Lake Almond with my mother."

Adair wanted to ask the girl about her mother, but decided against it.

They walked in silence before eventually coming upon a clearing with a small, oval lake. The sun reflected off its crystal-clear waters and the almond trees that surrounded it could be seen reflected in the water. A small smile found its way to Halona's lips as she stared at the area's reflection in the water.

◇•◇•◇

Halona ran and splashed through the water. Her mother, Elexia, chased behind her. The two ran and laughed as Halona tried to avoid being captured.

"I'm gonna get you!" Elexia shouted, her red curls bouncing as she waded through the water after her six-year-old.

"No, you won't, Mama!" Halona giggled. Suddenly, the young girl tripped and fell onto her hands and knees. Blood slowly trickled from her knees and palms as Elexia scooped the girl into her arms.

"It's alright, Little One." Elexia kissed her daughter's forehead. "I'll make it better."

She carried Halona to the bank where a brown bag waited. She searched through the bag for her healing paste. She rubbed the liquid on her daughter's palms and knees. Elexia's hands began to glow as she touched each of Halona's scrapes. In a matter of seconds, the tiny girl's cuts were healed and she was giggling again. She stood and rushed back into the water.

alona snapped out of her thoughts as a hand waved in front of her face. She looked to see Adair standing to her side, looking confused.

"What are we supposed to be getting for Mariana?" he asked.

"Oh!" Halona shook herself back into the present and pulled the list from the pocket of her trousers. "Let's see—we need Draccoves, Umaper, Esbi, Iberan, and some other herbs."

Adair stared at her, dumbfounded. She laughed at his obvious cluelessness. "I'll show you. You have to be careful when looking for herbs because some look like poisonous plants."

She bent down and pointed to a small plant. It was dark green with a red stripe running through its leaves. "This is Lirrea Grass. It's poisonous." She laughed when she saw Adair back away. "It's not deadly, but when eaten, it causes severe vomiting and pain."

She searched until she found another plant. It looked almost exactly like the Lirrea Grass. "This," she said with a smile, "is Algon. It is an herb used for treating stomach aches and nausea in pregnant women."

She plucked several, dropping them into the basket.

Adair picked one and stared at it. "It looks the same as the poisonous one," he frowned and twirled the Algon in his fingers.

Halona shook her head. "Look closer," she said, pushing his hand closer to his face. "The red lines are dashed instead of solid. I told you, it's the details that matter. One mistake could kill someone."

He shook his head and tossed the herb back into the basket. He sat by the bank of the lake as he watched Halona walk around and pick herbs, avoiding the poisonous plants. He laid back in the grass to nap, but sat up quickly when he heard her scream.

He ran to her and frowned when he saw her staring at a purple flower.

"You screamed because of a dumb flower?" He crossed his arms and frowned at her.

Halona looked up at him and shook her head. "This isn't a dumb flower. This is a White Ecelot."

"But it's purple." Adair blinked. He had always thought she was crazy. Now, he was positive that she was insane.

"It's supposed to be. The White Ecelot is purple during the day and white under the moonlight. It's said to have amazing healing properties and it is extremely rare. I've never seen one before."

"Then pick it and let's continue with gathering other things," he groaned.

Halona shook her head.

"No, a White Ecelot can only be used right after being picked. It must be fresh. If it is dried like other herbs it becomes deadly."

Adair groaned again and turned to walk back to the lake. Halona continued to stare at the flower.

Adair laid back down on the bank of the lake and took another nap. He awoke an hour later to see Halona standing over him with her hands on her hips.

He laughed as he sat up. "You finished?" He rubbed the sleep from his eyes.

She nodded and showed him the basket filled to the brim with plants. He nodded and stood. "Then, let's go."

"I want to make a side stop," she said with a sheepish smile.

"Fine, but don't take forever." Adair groaned.

"Since when are you the boss of me?" She frowned as she began walking around the right side of the lake.

Adair came to her side with a sigh. "Where are we going anyway?"

Halona smiled and looked over at him. "To visit someone."

She skipped along as she led him into the woods. She spotted a rainbow of colors from the corner of her eye. She laughed and ran toward the field of wildflowers. Adair sighed from behind her as she kneeled to pick a bouquet.

"I thought we were going to visit your friend." He frowned as he watched her.

"We are, but I want to take these to her," she smiled as she showed him the arrangement of purple and orange flowers. "These are her favorite."

Adair rolled his eyes and waited for the girl to finish her flower picking. She began skipping again as she held the flowers. Adair walked alongside her as his worry began to dissipate. She only had a small knife on her and if it came to a battle of strength, he could easily win.

Halona's pace began to slow as they walked through a natural archway created by the trees. The branches seemed to intertwine with one another above the duo's heads.

Adair expected there to be a hut nearby, but none was found. He stood under the archway while Halona continued into the small, secluded area. Trees surrounded the whole thing, creating walls and a ceiling of leaves. The sun shined through several holes in the treetops to illuminate the area. When he finished looking around, his eyes fell on Halona.

She kneeled at the base of the largest tree in the area. The flowers were beside her on the grass. Her mouth seemed to be moving as she spoke. That is when Adair noticed the small stone resting against the tree.

Suddenly, he began feeling a bit of remorse and guilt. He had been so terrible and impatient with her on the way. He had thought this was a trick to attack him, but really, she wanted to visit her deceased friend. Slowly, he walked to her side and kneeled beside her.

She turned her head to give him a small smile, but he could tell that she had been crying. Growing within the tree's large roots, near the headstone, were a bow and a quiver of arrows. Another bouquet of flowers rested by the stone.

"Your friend was an archer?" He ran his fingers along the intricate, floral pattern carved into the bow and each arrow.

Halona nodded as a few more tears dripped from her eyes. "She was the best in the clan. She's the reason that I became an archer. She trained me for years."

Adair pulled his hand away from the bow and looked down at the stone. The name across it read "Elexia."

"From what I've seen, you're quite the sharp shooter," he laughed as he wiped her tears with the sleeve of his cloak.

She chuckled and nodded, "She practically beat it into me. I could never leave training unless I hit at least one bullseye. I started to push myself harder once she was gone."

She reached down and traced the name on the stone. She ran her fingers along the dried petals of the older bouquet of flowers as she placed the new one on the opposite side of the stone.

"Who do you think left these flowers?" Adair looked over at her.

"Probably my father." She pointed to a green ribbon that tied the flowers together. "He always ties flowers for Mother with a green ribbon."

Adair's eyes widened as he stared at the stone. This was the grave of her mother! Adair could not imagine what he would do if he lost his own mother, but Halona had been living for what seemed like years without hers.

"Why green?" He glanced to the side.

"Her eyes," Halona smiled. "Father always said that her green eyes were mischievous and enchanting."

"Like yours?" Adair blurted without thinking. Halona's face turned pink as he began sputtering.

"I mean…" He tried to think of a coverup, but ended up going silent from embarrassment.

"We should, uh, head back," Halona suggested nervously. She muttered the prayer she had used earlier on Bennett's grave before standing.

Adair also stood, and the two returned to the village in silence.

Chapter 16

Halona smiled as the sunshine warmed her face. She and Adair ventured back to the lake the morning after visiting her mother's grave. Mariana sent them out to find and pick more herbs. The Moon Festival would start the next morning and the Mercants were due to arrive at any time.

They were sprawled out on the bank, finished with their assignment for a few hours when they decided to relax by the water of Lake Almond. Neither wanted to bring up Adair's comment from the day before. They lay in silence until a scream broke through the air. The two quickly stood. Halona snatched her bow and tossed Adair a small dagger that she had kept hidden in her boot. He still was not allowed to touch his weapons.

They raced through the woods and toward the sound. Eventually, they came upon a man within the wooded area near where Halona's mother was buried. His clothes were tattered and his blond hair and tan face were caked brown with mud. He bowed on his knees, begging to be spared.

Roka towered over the man. In his hands, he held a fresh bouquet of purple and orange flowers tied together with a green ribbon. He had a sword pointed at the man's throat.

"State your business," Roka ordered. His voice dripped with venom.

"Father!" Halona called out as she and Adair rushed toward the two men.

Roka gave the Peace Bringers a glance before pushing the blade of his sword closer to the man's throat.

The man's voice trembled as he attempted to speak. Fear caused the man's speech to come out incoherent. His eyes landed on the two young adults joining the savage leader and filled with joy as he turned to bow to Adair.

"Prince Adair, you're alive!" the man exclaimed happily.

Roka and Halona both gave Adair questioning looks. Roka sheathed his sword and pushed past the man to place the fresh flowers on his wife's grave and to make sure the bow and quiver were still in place.

"Who are you?" Adair asked, looking down at the man.

The stranger continued to bow. "Pardon my rudeness, Your Highness, I am Jameson. I am a soldier. Your father sent an army to search for you. The word is that Master Eyra told him you were safe, but your father would not believe him. He sent out an army to find you and we were caught in the storm two nights ago. I am the only survivor. I've been wandering around looking for shelter. This placed seemed as good as any."

Adair blinked in surprise. "Why did my father ignore Eyra's advice?" he asked.

The man's face took a solemn look. "Rumor has it that Queen Abry has fallen ill with grief. She believes you are dead. She is in a terrible state. King Roland believed that by bringing you home, she would be cured. Eyra is in prison for treason. He's awaiting a trial."

Adair's eyes widened and he grabbed the man by his shoulders. "My mother is ill? How bad is her condition?"

He continued to shake the man and prod him with questions. Halona put a hand on Adair's shoulder to keep him from shaking the man further.

"Adair, this man is injured. We need to get him help," she said softly.

Adair let the man go before nodding. "Fine, but when he is better, I want all the information he has about my mother."

Halona nodded in understanding and looked toward her father. He finished praying over Elexia's grave and was now watching the trio.

"Father." Halona began to speak, but stopped when her father raised a hand to silence her.

"He may come back to the village, but I want to make sure he is alone first," the Avory leader said as he stared down the injured man. "I want him to take us to his comrades."

The man's eyes widened, but he gave the Avory leader a frantic nod. Slowly, the man led the group to a secluded part of the woods.

A loud gasp erupted from Halona's mouth when she saw the devastation. Bodies were everywhere. Mud caked the ground all around them. The area had flooded during the storm and taken the army out. Several trees had fallen over and many unlucky men were crushed beneath them. She turned to look at Adair whose face was contorted in horror.

The prince's fist clenched as he turned to Roka, "I need to get in contact with my father. This army failed, but that will not stop him from sending another. If that happens, your village could be in danger. We both care about the lives of our people. Let me visit my father."

Roka shook his head, "I cannot allow you to leave on your own. I will allow you to write to your father, but that is it. I will send a messenger to carry and deliver the letter."

Adair wanted to protest, but knew it was unwise. Roka was being generous enough to allow him contact with his father through a letter. Adair knew better than to complain.

The group carefully made their way back to the village. Because the medical hut was still being rebuilt, Jameson, the injured Arian man, was taken to Roka's home to be healed by Halona and Mariana.

Chapter 17

dair awoke at sunrise to the sound of trumpets. Startled, he jumped out of bed and headed for the window. Evian was already awake in the bed across the room.

"The Mercants are here," the sleepy savage mumbled as he rubbed his eyes. He dragged himself out of bed to begin dressing for the day. He noticed Adair's confused form standing at the window watching as a large parade of people passed by.

"They're here for a festival, correct?" Adair looked over at the Halona's brother.

Evian nodded. "Yeah, the Moon Festival starts today and will go on for a couple of days. Don't expect to have any peace and quiet until the Mercants leave. When they party, they party hard."

Adair shook his head with a chuckle as he began to dress himself. "Good to know."

Once he and Evian were dressed, the two left the room they shared to head into the main room of Roka's home. Halona was already awake and leaning over the couch healing the man from the night before. The man was panting heavily as she worked her magic.

"How is he?" Adair spoke as he appeared behind her. He looked at the man from over her shoulder.

"Jameson will be fine. Mariana and I just have to make sure that he doesn't get an infection," she said as she placed a wet cloth on the man's forehead.

Mariana stepped into the room carrying a tray of bowls. "Breakfast anyone?"

Halona took two bowls from the tray and gave one to the man on the couch.

"Thank you, ma'am." He nodded as he sat up to eat.

Halona gave him a warm smile as she handed Adair and Evian their food. The three of them stood at the window watching the procession of Mercants enter the village. Roka and Liam were already at the town square to greet the village's guests.

"What happens during the Moon Festival?" Adair asked.

"It depends on the time of year," Evian explained. "Each year, the time of the Moon Festival is predicted by clan prophets. During our New Year celebration, the prophets determine what days the moon will be at its biggest and brightest. Then we plan a festival for those days."

Halona joined the two men at the window and continued from where Evian had left off, "Usually activities are decided by the season and the weather, but there is always lots of food, ale, and trading."

Adair watched as people began to set up tents and tables around the village. He could not help but feel excited for the festival. He had never experienced a festival as a participant. All the festivals in Aria were spectacles for the Royal family to watch.

"This will be interesting," he said, chuckling to himself.

Halona nodded and turned to look at the prince. "Mariana offered to stay here and watch Jameson so I can show you around the festival."

Adair turned to Mariana. She gave the young man a smile before glancing out the window. "The opening ceremony should start soon, you three better hurry if you want a good view."

Halona laughed as she grabbed Adair and Evian by the wrists and snatched a brown satchel from a chair before hauling the men from the house. She continued to pull on their arms until they were in the town square.

Adair could not believe his eyes. The amount of people in the tiny space was incredible. People were laughing and dancing along to music from the street performers. Trading was going on all around them at the tables and tents. Children were running and playing with fake swords and the smell of baked goods filled his nostrils.

He heard Halona laugh. She asked, "Isn't it incredible?"

Adair nodded with a smile. "I've never seen anything like it. I've never been on the inside of a festival. The Royal family in Aria usually just watches from the palace or special seating in the city."

Halona's mouth turned upward into a grin. "You should change that when you're King."

Adair laughed. "I just might have too."

Halona snatched his hand with a laugh. "Come on!"

They left Evian behind. She tugged on Adair's arm and dragged him to a table that was selling food. Different breads and colorful jars of jams covered the table. Halona smiled at the hefty, brown-eyed woman.

"Ah, Halona, what brings ya to me stand?" The woman gave the small girl a hard pat on the back.

Halona laughed and pointed to the barrel of ale resting on the ground. "Two ales, please."

The woman gave the girl a wink as she poured two glasses. "Be careful, dearie. This year's batch is a strong one."

Halona took the glasses and handed one to Adair before fishing two metal coins from her pocket. She placed them in the woman's hand and waved as she dragged Adair away.

"Goodbye, Rena!" she called as she and Adair disappeared into the crowd.

Halona found a bench to sit at and ushered Adair to the spot. She sat down and took a large gulp of her drink. She glanced at Adair to see he was staring at the drink.

"Am I going to get roaring drunk from this?" He looked at her.

Halona let out a soft laugh as she shook her head. "Not from one glass."

Adair nodded and took a sip. The sudden sweet taste that hit his tongue surprised him. It was warm and malty with a taste like freshly-baked bread. He took another sip and then another. Before long, his glass was empty. He looked over at Halona to see her stifling a laugh. He raised an eyebrow for an explanation, but she shook her head.

"What do you want to do now?" She asked as she took the glass from him and placed both glasses in a barrel beside the bench.

"What else is there to do?" He looked around at the tents and tables, waiting for something to catch his eye.

"We can go do some trading and then we could go watch the games," she suggested as she stood. Adair nodded and rose with her.

"Sounds fine to me." He stretched before following her through the crowd. Halona had a tight grip on his wrist to keep him from getting lost in the sea of people.

"If something stands out to you, let me know and we can stop," she instructed.

Adair nodded as his eyes searched the stalls that the two passed. The sea of goods never seemed to end. Every table or tent that he and Halona went by had something different. There were multiple traders selling furs, but each one had different types of furs from different areas. He laughed softly to himself as Halona stopped at a fur table to look at a vest.

"Don't you have enough of those?" Adair pointed to the vest she was trying on. It was as white as snow and as soft as a cloud.

"You can never have enough vests," she teased.

"My mother says the same thing about shoes," Adair muttered causing her to laugh.

Halona looked at herself in the tall mirror beside the table and smiled.

"I'll trade it to ya for that nice-lookin' ring on ya finger." The stout man behind the table spoke.

Halona looked down at the gold ring on her right hand. The sun reflected off the emerald stone. She did not hesitate to deny the offer. She removed the vest and snatched Adair's hand before dragging him away.

"You didn't want it?" He questioned as they began walking toward a tent.

She shook her head, "I'm not willing to part with my mother's ring for a silly vest."

"Ah," Adair hummed as they entered the tent.

The tent was larger on the inside than it seemed from the outside. Racks of clothing were set up along the sides and a tall, slender man with dark skin and a bushy black beard stood at the far end of the tent at a table. He smiled and waved to the duo as they entered and began looking around.

Adair watched as Halona scanned the women's clothing. He peered over her shoulder as she picked up a top off one of the racks. The colors were vibrant with many strange geometrical shapes.

"That is interesting," he laughed from behind her.

Halona nodded and laughed, "I can't believe that is a piece of clothing for everyday use. It hurts my eyes just to look at it."

Halona put the top back and pulled another from the rack. She blinked and felt the soft fabric between her fingers. She held it up closer to the light. The shirt only had one sleeve and it stopped at the midriff. The fabric was white, but had a pink belt sewn into the bottom.

Adair reached out and felt the fabric with his fingers. He watched as Halona held the top up to her body in front of a mirror.

"We have a small changing area if you would like to try that on," the Mercant man called out to her. He pointed to the right side of the tent where it extended into a separate room. A large sheet covered the entrance. Halona glanced at Adair. He gave her a small nudge toward the dressing area.

Adair pulled a dress off the rack and handed it to her. "You might as well try this on too." His face flushed as he spoke.

Halona laughed and rolled her eyes. "Yes, Sir."

Adair scanned through some of the men's clothing while he waited for Halona to finish changing. Nothing seemed to stand out to him, but he had an idea.

"Halona," he called out. "I will be right back!"

"Where are you going?" She shouted from behind the curtain.

"Don't worry about it," he laughed as he exited the tent.

Halona sighed as she left the changing room in the white top. She frowned at the way the shirt felt on her body. She made a few ridiculous poses in the mirror and twisted her body to make the coins chime. She was in her own little world until she heard a laugh come from behind her. She turned to see Adair smiling as if he was hiding something. Halona raised an eyebrow at him, but did not say anything.

"Don't look at me like that," he scolded teasingly. "Go put on the dress."

Halona rolled her eyes, but complied. Adair turned back to the men's clothing to look while he waited.

"Adair," he heard Halona's soft voice behind him. He turned to see her standing in the dress he had handed to her. The dress had a high collar. The olive-green fabric fell just above the floor and the tight sleeves extended down to her wrists where the fabric opened out. An auburn belt hung loosely around her waist.

Halona blinked as she watched the young prince gape at her. She spoke his name once more with a harsher tone to get his attention.

"You look…" His voice cracked as he spoke. "Good."

Halona said nothing as she gave herself a onceover in the tent's mirror. Her fingers ran through her hair as she undid the braid to let the red locks flow down her shoulders.

"I look like her," she whispered softly. "I look just like my mother."

She felt her eyes swelling with tears. Before Adair could notice, the Avory Princess was back in the changing area. She took great care as she replaced the dress on the hanger. She re-braided her hair after dressing and returned to the main area of the tent.

Adair pretended to keep himself occupied as the girl returned to his side. She placed the dress and top back onto the rack before roughly grabbing his wrist.

"Let's go somewhere else," she rasped. She paid no attention to the thing he was hiding behind his back.

Adair blinked and turned to look at the abandoned dress, but he nodded as she led him from the tent and to a bench. She sat down and took a deep breath. Halona wiped the tears from her eyes and took another deep breath. She closed her eyes and let her head fall against Adair's shoulder.

"It's hard, you know," she sniffled. "Losing someone that close to you."

"I know," Adair whispered as he placed something in her lap.

Halona's eyes opened and widened when she saw the white vest on her lap.

"You didn't," she gasped as she put it on. She ran her fingers over the soft fur.

"I did." Adair laughed.

"What did you trade for it?"

"That isn't important," Adair said and gave her a smile. "Don't worry about it."

"Thank you, Adair." She returned the smile as she stood. She grabbed his hand once more and began dragging him around the festival again.

He followed Halona as she led him through more of the festival. They passed more clothing tents as well as tables with weapons. Adair stopped in his tracks in front of a weapons' table. His abrupt stop caused Halona to jerk to a halt. She nearly fell over, but quickly regained her balance. Irritated, she turned to Adair to demand an explanation, but he was gone. She soon found him talking to a Mercant woman who happened to be selling weapons.

"Adair," she sighed as she came up to him from behind. "My father would kill you if you bought a new sword."

She knew he was holding something, but due to their differences in height she could not see it.

Adair shook his head with a chuckle, but did not say a thing. He rotated his body so she could see what was in his hands. He held up a dark-colored bow. From where she stood the bow looked simple, but as she looked closer she noticed the carvings. To Adair the carvings were nothing but beautiful symbols, but Halona knew them to be much more than that.

"This here bow tells the story of the Moon Spirit," the seller explained with a large smile.

Halona nodded as her fingers traced the symbols on the dark wood.

Adair concentrated on translating the symbols into the letters that Halona had taught him. There was one word that was the easiest for him to translate.

"Halona," he turned to the girl to speak. "Why is your name on this bow?"

Halona did not answer as she ran her fingers over the symbols that spelled her name. The Mercant seemed shocked by the young prince's question.

"Stupid boy, you should know by now that the Moon Spirit was named Halona. Have your parents taught you nothing, or did you just not pay any attention to your lessons?" The woman spat bitterly.

Halona lifted her head from inspecting the bow to scowl at the woman.

"Adair is not from the Avory clan," she hissed. "You should not speak so disrespectfully to a Peace Bringer."

The woman went silent as she watched Halona brush Adair's dark bangs from his face to reveal the diamond birthmark on his forehead. The woman gasped before lowering her head in apology.

Adair stood awkwardly between the two women as several others around the group began to whisper amongst themselves. Halona frowned before grabbing Adair's hand once more and dragging him away.

"Is this going to be how today goes?" Adair sighed. "Because I would actually like to stay at a stand for more than a few seconds."

"Too bad," Halona huffed as the two of them pushed through the crowd.

Adair sighed once more as he came to a halt, causing Halona to stop as well. Adair looked down at the savage girl and placed his hands on her shoulders.

"Are you alright?" he asked sincerely. "You're acting strange."

Halona nodded with a sigh. Adair took his hands from her shoulders before grasping her hands in his.

"Then let's go to another stand." He smiled as he pointed to a table with wooden crafts.

Halona glanced up at him with a smile of her own. "Lead the way."

The two found themselves sitting on a bench by the end of the day. Halona was repeatedly stroking her vest.

"What does your name mean anyway?" Adair glanced at her.

Halona stopped her stroking to smile up at the moon that was beginning to appear as the sky grew darker.

"Brightest light."

Chapter 18

Halona huffed as she frowned at Adair, water dripping from her hair and clothes. Her arms were crossed and she was screaming obscenities at the young man. Adair laughed at the girl. He guffawed long and hard which only irritated Halona more.

"I can't believe that you think this is funny!" She shouted as she stomped over to him and jabbed a pointed fingernail into his chest while she continued to curse.

Adair continued to laugh. His laughter distracted him. He did not notice Halona's face turning red. She brought her hands up to his shoulders and used his distractedness as an opportunity to shove him into the lake.

She grinned as she watched him fall into the water with a large splash. His messy, dark hair stuck to his face and his clothes soaked up water. He frowned as he grabbed her ankle to pull her down.

Halona let out a high-pitched shriek as she crashed into the water and fell on top of the prince. The two began laughing hysterically.

"You look ridiculous," he snorted as he watched her try to pull her wet hair from her eyes. It had fallen over the front of her face to make her look like a small, fuzzy monster. The thick, red locks tangled as she tugged them away from her face. She had no luck getting them out of her face and she gave up with a frown. Adair chuckled as he carefully removed the heavy hair from her face.

"Thanks," she mumbled as her cheeks flushed red. Adair thought nothing of it.

"We should head back. It will be dark by the time we get there." Halona pointed to the pink and orange sky. The sun had begun setting over the horizon.

Adair nodded and slowly stood up. He offered her his hand which she gratefully took. He helped her to her feet and they stood, holding hands. Both of their faces flushed and Adair quickly let go of her hand.

"Um, let's go," he spoke nervously. Halona nodded and turned to walk from the water. Her foot tangled in the weeds underwater and she came crashing down toward the surface. She braced herself for an impact that never came. When she opened her eyes, Adair was standing over her. His arm was around her waist.

"You really should be more careful, you clumsy fool," he said with a smirk as he helped her to her feet.

"I am not a fool," Halona spat with a frown. She brought her foot down onto his in a quick and painful stomp.

Adair groaned as he fell over into the water. Halona had already begun walking toward the basket of herbs on the bank of the lake when Adair regained his composure.

"Hey! Wait for me!" He shouted as he ran after her.

Mariana tapped her foot impatiently as she stared at the two twenty-year-olds standing before her. Water dripped from their hair and clothes.

Halona gave her mentor a nervous laugh as she handed her the basket of herbs. Mariana took them and retreated into the newly built medical hut. Halona and Adair followed. Halona glanced around the new hut. If she had not known that the hut was a pile of rubble just days before, she would not have believed that this was an entirely new building. The rooms were in the same layout and the main examination room looked the same as before. Several cots lined the center while jars and boxes filled the shelves and cabinets covering the walls. Jameson was resting on a cot in the corner.

"Go change into dry clothes," Mariana ordered the young adults. Halona nodded obediently and rushed from the medical hut with Adair on her heels.

"What was wrong with her?" Adair asked as they walked along the village road to Roka's home.

Halona glanced over at Adair, "Mariana always gets a little cranky around this time of year. She hates when the weather starts to get warmer at the beginning of summer. It reminds her of the day her son died."

"She had a son?" Adair seemed surprised that Mariana had children of her own. She was always so motherly to Halona and her brothers.

Halona nodded, picking at the fabric on her pants. "He was a several years older than me. He died when our village was raided by another clan."

Adair nodded, noticing the girl's discomfort. "Is that how your mother died?"

Halona stopped walking and nodded. She pulled her arms around herself. "Yeah, the raid was unexpected. My mother and I had been out walking around the village. I was nine."

Adair watched Halona as she rubbed her arms with her hands. He walked alongside her until they reached the house. He held the door open for her and they walked inside. The heat of the fire instantly warmed their shivering bodies. Halona disappeared into a back room for several minutes before returning in dry clothes and carrying a bundle in her hands.

"Here," she handed Adair the bundle of dry clothes. "We don't want you getting sick and dying on us."

Adair rolled his eyes as he took the clothes and headed to the room that he shared with Evian to change. No one else seemed to be back from their daily activities.

Halona sat in one of the thickly padded chairs and wrapped a blanket around herself. She stared down at the beautiful blue and green pattern knitted into it.

"Mama, why are you always doing that?" A five-year-old Halona peaked over the arm of the chair to stare at her mother. Elexia was knitting in her favorite chair.

"Because I like to do it," Elexia smiled at her youngest. "Do you want to learn?"

Halona shook her head several times. Her curly hair bounced around. "Nope, it looks boring."

Elexia laughed and set her knitting to the side before scooping the young girl up in her arms. Halona squealed as her mother left several kisses all over her face.

"Mama!" She protested. Elexia laughed as she cradled her daughter for several more minutes before Halona wiggled from her arms to go find one of her brothers to bother.

"I really should have let her teach me," Halona whispered to herself as she ran her fingers along the blanket.

Adair returned from the back room to see Halona staring down at the blanket she was curled up in. He started to take a few steps toward her, but before he could ask anything, the door burst open.

Roka stepped inside followed by Liam. The two were having a very animated conversation.

"I do not think it is a good idea. The clans are already strong allies. A marriage is not necessary, especially a marriage between those two. They hate one another. They would both be miserable," Liam was explaining.

Roka shook his head and opened his mouth to speak. His eyes landed on Halona lying on the chair. Adair stood awkwardly in the center of the room. He cleared his throat before sitting in a different chair.

"We'll talk more, Liam, when the Orasi arrive," Roka said to his son. His eyes did not leave Halona.

She looked up at her father and gave him a small smile. "Hi, Father," she whispered. Roka gave her head a small pat before heading into another room.

Liam flopped his body down on one of the larger chairs with a sigh. Halona gave her brother a questioning glance.

"What is wrong with you?" she chuckled.

Liam groaned before looking back at the door their father had gone through. When he felt like the coast was clear, he leaned close to Halona.

"Father is thinking about setting up a marriage between us and the Orasi," he whispered.

"Why?" She glanced back at the door and then to her brother. "Our relations with them are fine. We don't need a marriage to align us."

Liam shrugged his shoulders, "I think it is a good idea in thought, but not in practice."

"Who is he wanting to get married?" She sat up in the chair.

Liam bit his lip nervously before speaking. "You and Callahan," he said and flinched as he waited for her to explode.

Every emotion present in Halona's face immediately turned to anger. "Callahan?" she spat venomously.

Liam gave her a small nod as he leaned away. He knew about her relationship to the Orasi heir and he was not about to be in the line of her wrath. The two had been at odds with one another since they were children when Callahan lit one of Halona's dolls on fire.

"Who is Callahan?" Adair asked, watching the siblings.

"The heir to the Orasi clan. He is a pompous asshole who has no respect for other people. He is constantly looking down on others because he thinks he is the Moon's greatest gift to the world. He makes me want to vomit," Halona ranted.

Adair shook his head with a laugh. "He sounds wonderful."

Halona frowned and crossed her arms before shaking her head.

Liam laughed and glanced at Adair, "Halona has tried to kill him on several occasions. It's a wonder that our clan and the Orasi remain such good allies."

Halona threw a pillow at her brother's head. It bounced off the side of his face and landed in his lap. Liam retaliated by launching the pillow back. Halona picked it up to throw it again, but stopped when Roka returned from one of the other rooms.

Roka raised his eyebrow at his daughter. She was crouched in the chair with a pillow poised over her head. She gave him a small smile before launching the pillow at Liam. Roka shook his head with a deep chuckle as he watched Liam throw the pillow back at his sister.

"Don't break anything," he said, and took a spot on one of the open chairs.

Halona caught the pillow, but instead of throwing it, she turned to her father. "You want me to marry Callahan?"

Roka frowned and glanced at Liam who chuckled nervously before sinking down into the chair. Roka turned his attention to Halona. "It is merely a suggestion that I am going to make during the meeting with the Orasi. They should arrive in a few days for the yearly meeting."

Halona opened her mouth to protest, but Roka cut her off.

"It is only a suggestion, Halona. It is by no means a final decision. I have yet to discuss it with Elias."

Halona sighed and threw the pillow back at Liam to relieve her frustration. The front door of the house opened once more as Severin and Evian stepped through the threshold. As usual, Evian was bloody and bruised from the brothers' daily sparring. A large, purple bruise was forming around his left eye. His bottom lip was swollen and cracked with dried blood. The biggest injury, however, was on Evian's right arm. It was in a sling and bandaged. Blood was already turning the bandages red.

Halona stood with a glare at both of her brothers. "Evian," she growled and pointed at the bandage wrapped around his arm.

Evian let out a nervous chuckle as he tried to hide behind his older brother, "I'm fine. Mariana took care of it."

"Where is she?" Roka spoke as he strode to his sons to inspect the damage done to Evian's arm.

"She had some things to take care of back at the medical hut. She said that dinner may be late tonight unless someone else wants to cook," Evian shrugged.

"I'll make dinner tonight," Halona offered.

Her selfless suggestion was quickly rejected with a chorus of no's! Halona frowned, offended, and crossed her arms.

"My cooking is not that bad," she said, sulking.

"Your cooking is so bad even a boar wouldn't eat it," Evian pretended to retch at the thought of eating Halona's cooking.

Roka stood and headed for the kitchen. He ruffled Halona's hair as he walked by her. "I will make dinner tonight. We need the house to stay standing," he said.

"Thank the Moon!" Evian exclaimed as he fell to his knees. "We're saved."

Halona frowned and pulled her shoe from her foot before launching it at Evian. She hit her target on the forehead. Evian dropped to the floor as he groaned in pain.

The commotion had gone unnoticed by Roka because he had already made it to the kitchen. Evian continued to hold his head from his spot on the floor. Halona grinned, pleased with herself. Severin ignored his younger brother's pain as he stepped over him to find a seat. The room went quiet for several minutes until Adair spoke up with a question.

"Is Mariana your step-mother?" Adair asked innocently. He meant no harm in the statement. He had no idea that his simple question would provoke glares and death threats. The glare and murderous intent that radiated off Severin in the room confused him. Liam frowned, but showed no intention of harming the prince, and Evian scoffed as he turned his attention to his wound.

"No," Severin scowled. He stood to make a move toward the young man, but Halona grabbed his arm to stop him.

"Severin, he didn't mean it," she whispered lowly. Severin pulled his arm from her grasp and pushed past her to get to the prince. He grabbed the front of Adair's shirt and yanked him forward.

"Care to ask that again?" Severin glowered. His usual calm disposition was gone and replaced with nothing but anger. Adair stared, confused, at the man. How had he offended him? He was only asking a simple question.

Halona rose to her feet and pushed herself in between her brother and Adair.

"Severin, stop. He didn't mean it," she said and looked at her brother. Her short stature made it difficult for her to make a difference in the squabble. Severin was taller than she and Adair. He could have easily pushed his sister out of the way. Adair stood behind Halona, looking puzzled while she continued to defend him.

"What did I do? I did not mean anything rude by it." Adair looked into Severin's eyes for a moment as he spoke. He turned from the older man and looked to Halona for an answer.

Halona continued to try to keep Severin from attacking Adair. She held her ground between the two men. After several minutes of staring down Adair and his sister, Severin backed away.

"What was that about?" Adair whispered to her. She grabbed him by the arm and dragged him to a different area of the room.

"You insulted our mother," she said simply.

"What? How? That was not my intention." He shook his head vigorously while staring at her in disbelief.

Halona nodded, "We don't believe in remarrying after a spouse dies."

Adair's dumbfounded expression remained, so Halona began to explain.

"Marriage is very important to us. In fact, I would go so far as to say that marriage is sacred to us. By remarrying someone else, you are disrespecting your deceased spouse and the times you shared together. By asking if Mariana was our step-mother, you implied that our mother's memory is not sacred to us or our father and she deserves to be forgotten."

Adair blinked and nodded as he began to understand. He turned to the other men in the room and bowed. "I'm sorry. I didn't know."

Halona gave him a tiny smile and a firm pat on the back. "I know, but now you do. Try not to make that mistake again. Severin might actually kill you next time."

"I'll keep that in mind," Adair sighed. "I'm just baffled as to why Mariana is always here cooking and caring for your family."

Halona chuckled, "It is a little strange, and it isn't normal, but Mariana made a promise to take care of us if anything happened to our mother. Mariana has always been an aunt-like figure to us. Even before Mother died, Mariana spent considerable time with our family."

Adair nodded. He still did not know how he would handle losing his mother. Halona seemed to be doing well, but it had been years since her mother's death. If Adair were to lose his mother, he felt he would go insane without any hope of recovery.

Chapter 19

Halona had left the medical hut to change into nicer clothes for the meeting with the Orasi that was to occur that night. While she was gone, Adair watched as Mariana organized the herbs into special jars and containers.

"Would you like some help, Mariana?" Adair offered.

Mariana turned around and offered Adair a large smile. "Thank you, dear."

The prince dipped his head and stood to help the older woman organize the herbs. He remembered some of what Halona taught him about each of them. He knew none were poisons, but he could only identify a few herbs.

He focused on the herbs that he knew and helped Mariana organize them into specific piles.

"Put about a quarter of each herb into separate piles. I will create pastes out of them," she instructed.

Adair silently organized the herbs into boxes with Mariana. Occasionally, he had to ask about the name of an herb, but he did a decent job with his limited knowledge.

"Halona taught you about the herbs?" Mariana glanced at Adair, impressed.

He nodded as he placed the final herb into its container.

Mariana smiled. "She seems to have taken a liking to you."

Adair laughed softly. "I suppose I don't hate her as much as I used too."

Adair did not notice the small smirk playing on Mariana's lips as she spoke, "You've changed quite a bit since we found you all those weeks ago."

Adair chuckled. "This has been an interesting experience."

"I'm sure you miss your family." Mariana began placing the lids on the boxes before arranging them on the counters with labels.

Adair nodded with a sad expression. "I do. I learned that my mother was so worried that she had fallen severely ill. I can't imagine what I would do if she passed."

Adair helped Mariana reach the top shelves to place some boxes there.

Mariana smiled and patted the young man's shoulder, "It takes adjustment when you lose someone as close as your mother. I stayed beside each of Elexia's children and even her husband after her passing."

Adair glanced her way. "You were close with their mother?"

Mariana nodded with a smile. "Elexia was my best friend. We were by each other's side for almost every important event of our lives. I was present for her wedding and the birth of each of her children. She and I even had a few adventures together."

Adair smiled sadly as he remembered his relationship with Bennett. He had no doubt that if Bennett were still alive, they would be uncles to each other's children. "How did you cope with losing Elexia?"

Mariana sighed and rested against the counter. "It was hard. I had nightmares for months. I kept blaming myself because I wasn't there. Eventually, I realized that there was nothing I could have done to prevent her death. She died protecting her child. I would have done the same for my own children. We believe that when someone dies, it is fate, yet, we behave as if we could have made a difference. It is irrational, but it was hard to stop imagining outcomes where Elexia would still be alive today."

The conversation ended as Halona entered through the door of the hut. She was no longer dressed in her usual rags, but instead wore a forest-green gown to match her eyes. The sleeves were long and the collar was high. The dress dragged the ground and covered her feet.

Halona sat in the chair that rested between the cots. She sighed and leaned back in a casual manner. She pulled her hair from its messy bun to let it fall down her shoulders in curly waves.

Mariana smiled at the young girl. "You should curl your hair more often. You look more like your mother when you do."

Halona rolled her eyes with a small smile. "I look like Mother anyway. Besides, it's easier to braid it."

"Have the Orasi arrived?" Mariana glanced out the window to see many people putting up decorations to welcome their greatest allies.

"They should be here soon. Father sent Severin and a few others out to meet them along their usual path. Everyone is running around like mad trying to get everything ready."

Mariana let out a hearty laugh. "Well of course. The Avory and Orasi have been allies for almost a century."

"Yes, I know," Halona groaned. "But when they visit, they bring Callahan."

"Callahan is part of the deal, Halona. He is the Orasi heir."

Halona groaned once more and mumbled under her breath.

Adair shook his head with a laugh as he remembered the meetings his father would have with the King of Etras.

Adair stepped into his family's throne room. He was dressed in an expensive, grey tailored suit. A blue tie around his neck was pitifully crooked. His mother smiled and brought him in for a warm embrace. He heard her laugh softly at his terrible attempt at the tie. She undid his work and began to smooth his errors.

"You and your father can never tie your ties properly." Queen Abry lightly teased her son.

Adair chuckled and nodded. "I had to get something from him."

Queen Abry laughed again as she finished the tie. "You look dashing, Adair. King Olric will be very impressed." She brushed a stray hair from his face.

Adair sighed. He understood the need to impress the King of Etras. King Roland and King Olric were signing a treaty to ensure peace would stay between the two countries even though they had been allies for over a century. Aria was by far the strongest of the three countries in Salacir and Etras needed the support from the stronger country to keep a rebellion that had been brewing in check.

King Roland made his way into the room and joined his wife and only son. He kissed his wife's forehead and gave Adair's shoulder a hard pat. It almost caused the teenaged prince to topple over.

◇•◇•◇

pale hand begin to wave in front of his face, bringing Adair from his memories.

"Hello, Adair. Are you even listening to me?" A slightly irritated grumble came from Halona's throat.

Adair's head shook as he snapped back to the present, "Uh. What? Huh?" He looked up at her, puzzled.

Halona sighed as her hand connected with her face in an exasperated gesture. "Princes," she grumbled.

Adair rolled his eyes at the girl. "Savages," he said with a groan to tease her.

She opened her mouth to retort, but before the words left her mouth she was interrupted by another hand on her shoulder.

Evian stood behind his sister with an unusually serious expression on his face. "The Orasi are here," he said. He glanced at Adair before looking back at his sister. "Are you ready?"

Halona sighed and slowly stood from her chair. She gave Adair an exasperated look before groaning which caused the prince to smirk. She smoothed her dress again and made sure that her hair looked presentable. Before she left the hut, she turned to Adair.

"Stay here with Mariana," she ordered.

Adair rolled his eyes and nodded. He glanced over at Mariana who smiled at Halona.

"Don't worry, dear. I'll put him to work." Mariana chuckled.

Satisfied, Halona turned toward her brother and plastered a believable smile on her face as they left the hut. The village streets were lined with flowers and banners. Lanterns lit the dark streets and musicians played merry tunes all around them. People filled the streets cheering as the Orasi's clan leader and his entourage filed through the streets to the village's main meeting house.

Halona and Evian slowly followed behind the group. Outside of the meeting house stood four men. She heard Evian mumble something about the Orasi leader bringing more guards than he needed. Halona rolled her eyes as they continued to walk forward.

"Halona, don't look so sour. You won't impress anyone when your face looks like a pouting fish," Liam teased as he appeared at his sister's side.

Halona rolled her eyes as she turned to her older brother and said, "Sorry, I just don't feel like dealing with Callahan's cocky ass. I get enough of that with Adair."

Liam let out a light chuckle. "Try not to injure him like last time."

Halona smiled and shook her head. "I am not promising anything. Shouldn't you already be inside?"

It was Liam's turn to roll his eyes. "I'm not always up Father's ass. He sent me to run an errand."

When the trio of siblings reached the meeting house, the guards outside showed their respect by placing their hands over their chests and bowing. The three siblings returned the gesture. After coming up from his bow, Liam gave one of the guards a suggestive wink. The guard chuckled as his lips curled into a small smile. Halona groaned softly to herself and leaned to whisper to her brother.

"Try to restrain yourself this year. We don't need another incident." She gave him a serious look.

"I was found naked in a tree *one* time." Liam frowned childishly.

Halona only rolled her eyes as they made their way into the building. They walked through the elaborate maze of hallways and eventually stopped in front of a large oak door. An Avory guard and an Orasi guard were standing outside of the office. They opened the door for the set of siblings.

Roka's office was large. In the center sat an oval table with enough chairs to hold his council. The floors and walls were made of colored stone.

Inside, Roka stood around the table with three others. One of the men was Severin. Halona, Evian, and Liam all bowed.

The oldest of the group was a tall, thin, man with a bushy, white beard. He stood with confidence as he and Roka spoke to one another. On either side of the bearded man were his children. His eldest son stood on his right while his daughter stood on the left.

Roka turned to his children with a nod as they circled the table with the others. The Orasi leader dipped his head in respect.

"Liam, you are looking well. I believe the last time I was here, you were ill," he spoke gruffly.

Liam nodded. "It is good to see you as well, Elias. I'm doing much better this year."

Elias nodded. His smile made him appear even older. He returned his attention to Roka as the two began speaking. Elias seemed shocked by Roka's words. He made several glances to his son and then to Halona.

"Marriage," Elias seemed surprised. "Between Halona and Callahan?" He looked toward Roka, hoping that he had heard the younger leader wrong.

"That seems like a dreadful idea," Elias responded to Roka's nod. "Even I know that my son and your daughter are not fond of one another."

Roka nodded. "So, I've been told."

Elias glanced around the room more. His eyes fell over each of the leaders' children as he formed a better idea. "Would you accept my daughter as a wife for one of your sons? Liam perhaps. That would surely strengthen our bond for more generations."

Halona snickered lightly as Liam's face paled. The eldest of Roka's children opened his mouth to speak, but his father spoke first.

"Elias, I'm sure you are already aware that Liam is not interested in marrying . . . a woman," Roka spoke clearly. Elias shook his head.

"I apologize. I was not thinking clearly," Elias said to the father and son. "But what of your other sons?"

Roka turned toward Severin and Evian before looking back at Elias. "I suppose that could be arranged, but only with their consent."

Halona's jaw dropped and she frowned. Her brothers were going to get the choice, but if it came down to it, her father would force her to marry anyone he wanted.

Liam sensed Halona's anger and grasped her arm to calm her. She glanced over at Elias's daughter, Lilith. The girl was Halona's age, but she seemed more mature. She kept her face void of any emotion that she may have felt by her father's marriage proposal. When asked what she thought about marrying one of the Avory leader's sons, she nodded. "I will do anything that would keep our clans bonded longer." Lilith stood tall as she spoke.

Halona frowned. She had never liked Lilith, and Lilith had never liked her. Halona found that she was always comparing herself to Lilith who was tall, had gorgeous brown locks, and brown eyes that could seduce anyone. Halona was much shorter, her red hair always nappy looking, and her seducing skills non-existent.

Lilith's brother, Callahan, caught Halona staring in their direction. He smirked before excusing himself from his father's side. When he came into Halona's view, her frown became larger.

Callahan was like his father in looks, but far from him in personality. Halona would not deny that Callahan was handsome, but she hated his arrogance. In her eyes, Callahan's gorgeous, blue eyes and practically flawless, brown hair did absolutely nothing to make up for his vulgar personality.

Halona hated being in the same vicinity as Callahan. When he walked over to join her and her brothers, she had to fight the urge to vomit on his shiny shoes.

"Look who finally decided to join the party," he said in a cocky tone.

"Buzz off, Callahan. I am not in the mood for your dumbassery," Halona snapped quietly. She knew their fathers could probably hear, but she did not give a damn. Liam snickered at the word "dumbassery" which earned him a quick glance from their father. He quieted down and sat in a chair to keep himself out of the upcoming dispute.

Callahan pretended to be hurt by Halona's comment. He pressed his hand to his chest as he spoke. "Halona, my darling, you hurt my feelings."

The girl scoffed and rolled her eyes. "First off, I am not your darling. Secondly, the only thing I will hurt is your pride and maybe your testicles."

Before she could allow Callahan to respond with a comment that would most likely make her hate the man even more, she went and sat in a chair beside Liam. Her brother gave her a pat on the head to congratulate her on controlling herself.

Callahan returned to his father's side and continued to speak with his sister and the leaders. Roka waved Liam over to the group.

Liam sighed and patted Halona's head again. "The official business is starting. Duty calls," he said with a laugh before heading to his father. Severin took Liam's seat between Halona and Evian.

"I don't see why we even have to be in here," Halona groaned with a whisper. "It's not like I have any chance of being leader."

Severin hushed his sister as the others joined them around the table to begin the meeting. Halona zoned out through most of it until she felt a pinch on her leg.

She sat up and looked toward Severin. "Pay attention," he whispered. "This is important for you."

Halona rolled her eyes as she began tuning into the conversation.

"I have sources that have informed me that the country of Etras as well as other clans are losing territory to the Ivane. They are expanding their borders and conquering whoever they come across," Callahan explained in a serious tone.

Roka turned to Elias, surprised. "Is this true?"

Elias nodded. "It's only a matter of time before they reach Orasi borders."

"We have plenty of warriors to defend ourselves, but I've heard that the Ivane have increased their numbers by enslaving those they've captured or by using men from their allies," Callahan added.

"Who are their allies?" Liam leaned forward.

Callahan shook his head. "We have not been able to figure that out."

Elias spoke once again. "I believe this may be a good time for Halona to begin searching for the other Peace Bringer. If a war begins, we are going to need the Peace Bringers."

"I've already found him," Halona said softly. "He is currently with Mariana."

Elias's eyes widened. "The second Peace Bringer has been found?" He turned to Roka for an explanation.

Roka nodded and began to explain the situation to the Orasi leaders. "His name is Adair. He is the son of Aria's King. He and his men stumbled upon our lands many weeks ago."

Elias grinned and pounded his fist on the table in joy. "Then he and his men can help."

Halona shook her head and glanced at the Orasi leader. "His men were wiped out by a few rogues from our village. Adair is the only survivor."

Roka added to Halona's words. "And the king is not fond of the idea that his son is in our custody. He sent an army to destroy the clan and retrieve the prince, but the Moon Spirit was on our side."

Elias sunk back in his seat as he stroked his beard in thought. "If a war is going to happen, maybe joining forces with the King of Aria would be a wise idea."

Callahan rose to his feet in frustration. "Absolutely not! Think of what they've done to our people in the past. They have sent armies to destroy us even when we are not the threat!"

Elias sent his son a stern look and Callahan reluctantly sat back down. His rage radiated as the meeting continued.

Hours later, the meeting came to a halt. It had been decided that soon, Adair would travel, with several others from the Orasi and Avory, to the capital to speak with the king about joining their forces. The end of the meeting meant that the two clans could embark on the yearly feast hunt. Elias and Roka both agreed to have Halona and Callahan go on their hunt together as a way to encourage them to work together and get along.

Once the meeting was dismissed, Halona returned to the medical hut. She slumped through the doors. Adair was relaxing on one of the cots as he wrote in a journal. He looked up and noticed Halona's moping.

"What is the matter with you?" He set the journal down and sat up.

"Tonight, is the Feast Hunt and I am being paired with Callahan." She frowned and collapsed onto another cot.

"What is the Feast Hunt?" Adair asked curiously.

"It's a tradition that we have whenever the Orasi visit. We pair up and go out to hunt game. Then we bring it back and prepare it for a large feast."

"That sounds interesting." Adair smiled.

"You can't go. You'll be staying with Mariana again."

Adair opened his mouth to protest, but was cut off by the sound of a horn. That was Halona's signal that it was time for her to go. Her face fell as she stood to exit the hut.

Callahan was waiting for her outside the hut. He motioned with his head for her to follow him. She huffed and walked past him so she was in the lead. If she had to do this, she was going to be the authority figure in their little group of two.

Slowly, groups of all sizes began arriving in the town square one by one. Besides the few guards left behind to protect the homestead, the children, elderly, and pregnant were the only ones not participating in the hunt. Halona's father and brothers were leading their own individual groups. Roka and Elias were hunting together like old friends. Halona noticed Liam and the handsome Orasi guard he had flirted with earlier. Because of her spacing, she fell behind Callahan as they walked to the rendezvous point where her father and Elias began the ceremonial speech in their clans' ancient languages.

She quickly found Callahan and joined his side. He gave her a cocky smirk when she returned.

"Don't get lost, Princess," he mocked. Halona rolled her eyes, but otherwise chose to ignore him.

As Roka and Elias's speeches neared the end, each person at the rendezvous point began pulling out their weapons.

Callahan stood beside Halona. "Lead the way, Princess." He smirked.

She took a deep breath and slowly began to walk ahead of Callahan. She knew the perfect spot to hunt. They had been given the job of hunting for an elk. Halona groaned inwardly as she led Callahan out of the village. She was not looking forward to this. Callahan gave her one more smirk as the lights from the village faded behind them. She wondered if she could get away with *accidentally* shooting Callahan with an arrow.

Chapter 20

alona groaned, sitting up in the darkness. Her head was pounding and her ankle was throbbing in pain. She scanned the area, looking for anything that might stand out. A large figure sat along the wall across from her. As her eyes began to adjust to the blackness around her, she recognized the figure. It was Callahan. His eyes slowly opened. He noticed her lying across from him. She blinked as she remembered how they had fallen.

After separating for the hunt, she had led Callahan through a small wooded area near the clan's border. They had quickly found an elk, but it evaded them. Halona knew a way that they could go around the forest and meet the elk on the other side. Unfortunately, it had been so long since her last hunt, Halona miscalculated the distance. Instead of coming up on the outside of the forest, the two managed to get lost in it. Their misfortune continued when a small earthquake rattled the ground under their feet causing the edge of the ground to crumble. They fell several feet down into a hole.

"Are you finally awake?" Callahan grumbled under his breath. Halona stood to try to walk to him, but her ankle gave out. She collapsed on top of him causing him to groan in pain.

"Sorry," she squeaked as she crawled to his side.

Callahan rubbed his stomach. "For being so small, you weigh a lot more than I expected."

Halona's jaw dropped and she punched the side of his face. He cried out in pain once more.

"I didn't mean that as an insult!" He frowned. "I was only saying that you weigh more than you look like you do. That should be a compliment."

She frowned and crossed her arms as she leaned against the wall of the hole. She said nothing as Callahan stood.

He pulled out two daggers and stabbed them into the walls of the hole. He tried using them to climb, but it only caused parts of the wall to crumble. Halona yelped in surprised as dirt, rocks, and Callahan came tumbling down. The debris filled the floor of the hole, creating a smaller floor space for the two of them. Callahan swore under his breath before trying to climb the collapsed wall of dirt. Again, the solid parts of the wall crumbled to the ground. He landed next to Halona with a very irate expression.

Halona tried turning her body away from the falling debris, but only hissed in pain from her injured ankle. Callahan raised an eyebrow and glanced down at her ankle. He reached out and took it to examine it. He poked it several times, causing Halona to cry out in pain. She was positive that he was doing it on purpose.

"It's not broken, but you won't be able to walk on it. You won't be able to climb out of this hole with only one foot." He sighed.

Halona huffed and frowned. "You couldn't climb out with two arms," she spat bitterly.

He closed his eyes, frustrated with the girl. "No, but if you hadn't led us in this direction, we wouldn't be in this mess."

She groaned, but deep down knew he was right. She had always been terrible at tracking and directions. She looked up at the moon through the opening hole and then the pile of dirt in front of them. She silently begged the Moon Spirit to help them. Instantly, she got an idea. She nudged Callahan with her arm and pointed to the dirt.

"Hey, if you made the rest of that wall collapse again, we might be able to climb the pile to get out."

"Are you out of your mind? It could crush you." He stared at her in disbelief.

"Since when do you care about my safety?" She raised an eyebrow.

"Good point." He nodded as he stood to try climbing again. Callahan began climbing the wall and he could feel it breaking apart beneath him. He looked down at Halona, waiting for her to stand. She kept all her weight on one foot and thanked the Moon for the sudden gift of balance. Once she was standing, he swung one of his feet into the wall. He and the wall came down creating a large cloud of dust. Neither of them could see anything. By the time the dust cloud settled, Halona was missing. Callahan shoved the dirt off and began looking around for the annoying redhead.

"Halona!" He shouted, hearing nothing but the sound of his voice echoing back at him. He yelled again and again, but there was no answer. He started digging around frantically. If he left without the Avory clan's princess and Peace Bringer, he would be a dead man. Finally, after what seemed like an eternity, a pale hand popped up out of the dirt. Halona managed to sit herself up. She coughed and shook the dirt out of her hair.

"I have dirt in places that I didn't think was possible," she said with a frown. Callahan snorted with laughter which earned him a clod of dirt to the face. He threw a clod back and then helped the girl to her feet. Halona winced from the pain in her ankle and leaned her body forward into Callahan's chest.

"Can you walk?" Callahan looked down at her as he carefully pushed her away from his chest. Usually, he would not mind having a girl clutching onto him, but this girl was Halona.

She frowned and gave him an annoyed look, "You just told me that I won't be able to walk."

Callahan chuckled nervously. "Yeah, I remembered."

"No, you didn't," she said and crossed her arms.

Callahan sighed. He helped her onto his back before beginning to climb up the large pile of dirt he had created.

"Hang on tight. I will carry you back," he grumbled. Halona did not protest. Instead, her arms wrapped around Callahan's shoulders.

◇•◇•◇

Chapter 21

Morning came without Halona and Callahan's return. Roka and Elias sat around the oval table in the meeting house with a few other men, including Halona's brothers.

"Perhaps we should send a group out to find them? Callahan has been known to wander during hunts," Elias suggested.

Liam nodded, concerned for his younger sister's safety. "Father, Elias is right. Maybe we should send someone out to find them. They could have gotten hurt in yesterday's earthquake."

Roka ran a hand through his dark hair. His usually hard expression was softer and worried.

"You are right," Roka said and looked to his oldest son. "Liam, you are in charge until I return. I am going to find those two and bring them back. If I do not return by morning, send a group out."

Liam nodded obediently. He wanted to be the one to find his sister, but orders were orders.

Roka stood and headed for the door. As he reached to open it, the door burst open. A scout rushed in. He was bloody and injured.

"Sir, we're under attack!" He panted heavily.

"Attack?" Roka looked at the man, concerned. He grabbed his long sword and axe from the table.

The man nodded. "Another clan is on their way. I could not get a good look at them, but I think their crest was that of the Itis."

Roka turned to the others in the meeting room. He did not say anything as he rushed from the room. His sons and guards rushed after.

"Father," Lilith looked toward Elias. His men looked to him as well. They were all waiting for orders.

"We are the Avory's allies. We will fight with them!" Elias grabbed his own longsword and pointed toward the door. His men rushed out and he stayed behind with Lilith. "Get somewhere safe, sweetheart," he said and kissed his daughter's forehead. He rushed from the room. Lilith ran after.

Lilith soon found Mariana ushering anyone who could not fight into a separate door to the meeting house. She was helping expectant mothers, children, and the elderly escape from the harm that could befall them. Lilith ran to help the older woman usher people inside. She looked up and saw rain clouds rolling in over the village.

"Take them to the basement," Mariana ordered. "Go down these stairs. Every time you come to multiple paths, take the path on the right."

Lilith nodded and finished getting the others down the stairs. She watched as Mariana ran back to the medical hut to meet up with a young man Lilith did not know. She shut and latched the door behind her before ascending down the stairs.

Mariana met Adair outside of the medical hut. "Mariana what is going on?" He looked toward the older woman for answers.

"The village is under attack. I know you can't heal, but I could use your help with anyone who comes injured. Halona and Callahan still have not returned."

Adair's face fell. Halona was not back yet? Was it possible the attackers had already gotten to them?

"We can only hope that they are safe, but we must be ready. We will have to go out there and help anyone we can. Bring your sword. You will need it," Mariana explained as she began throwing supplies into a bag. She pulled up a couple of floorboards in the hut to reveal Adair's sword. Adair grabbed it and headed for the door.

Roka stopped them as they exited the medical hut. He looked at Adair and then to the sword. He dipped his head in approval before exchanging words with Mariana.

"They are getting closer. I have sent men out to slow them down, but they are outnumbering us. You should get somewhere safe with the others. When the battle ends, you can heal the injured," Roka ordered.

"Sir, I refuse to sit back and wait while our men and women fall." Mariana frowned and clutched her bag. "I'm bringing Adair along to help."

Roka shook his head. "Mariana, this is an order. Halona still has a lot to learn about healing and she cannot learn from the best if the best and only healer we have is dead."

"I'm sorry, Sir, but this is one order that I will not follow." Mariana stood her ground.

Roka sighed as he knew he could not change Mariana's mind. A loud cry was heard throughout the surrounding forest. The sound of a loud war-horn filled the air.

Roka's head turned to the forest. He unsheathed his sword with a mighty war cry and headed into the depths of battle.

Adair turned to Mariana. She smiled at him as they charged into the forest. The grey clouds covering the area began to pour rain down onto the village and the battle field.

Chapter 22

"Really?" Halona shouted at the moon as she held her middle finger in the air. Had she been thinking clearly, she would have known that cursing her deity was a bad idea. Callahan scowled up at the girl as she voiced her displeasure. Not long after they climbed from the hole, it began to pour.

"Will you stop screaming?" Callahan barked. "A little water in your hair isn't bad. It will wash the dirt out."

Halona huffed. The rain was causing her long hair to stick to her face. She was still on Callahan's back as he ran back toward the village. He stopped suddenly and looked around.

"What?" Halona frowned. "Did you forget where we need to go?"

Callahan shushed her.

"Don't you shush me!"

"Shut up," he hissed as he covered her mouth with his hand. He quickly ducked behind several trees to provide cover for them. Halona frowned as she ripped his hand away from her face.

"What the hell, Callahan?" She scowled.

He shushed her again. "Listen."

Halona eye's narrowed as she listened to the sounds around them. The clashing of metal and shouting could be heard nearby.

"What is that?" she asked as she looked him over.

"That's the sound of a battle," he answered. His brow furrowed as he went deep into his thoughts.

Halona frowned as she began wondering why a battle would be occurring so close to the village.

"Maybe the Ivane skipped the Orasi all together and wanted to take us all out at once," Callahan said aloud. He shook his head and silently began to walk toward the sound with Halona still on his back.

Chapter 23

dair panted as he swung at another attacker. His sword buried itself into the man's shoulder. He gripped the hilt tightly as he brought it down through the man's chest. The man dropped to the ground, dead. Mariana, arm bleeding from an earlier attack, knelt over an Avory man with an injury to his leg. She was doing her best to heal it as fast as possible.

"Mariana, maybe you should have listened to Roka." Adair said as he swung at a female attacker. This time the sword sliced clear through the woman's abdomen.

Mariana shook her head as she finished healing the injured man. "No, I've saved too many people that would have died had I stayed away from the battle."

"Then at least tend to your wounds." Adair groaned as he deflected a blow from yet another attacker.

The man that Mariana healed stood and shakily grabbed his weapon. He charged back into battle.

Mariana's body shook as she tried to stand. She coughed, causing blood to spurt from her mouth. Adair rushed to her side.

"Mariana, you're using up too much energy. You need to go back to the village," he told her.

Just as Mariana was about to respond, Roka and Severin came barreling through the trees chasing after fleeing enemies.

"They've broken through the lines to the village!" Roka shouted. "We need to stop them there."

Severin nodded before throwing his sword like a javelin. It pierced into one of the fleeing men's backs, dropping him dead in an instant. Roka took care of the other man by using his shock to hack at his legs with his axe. The man's body toppled toward the ground where the Avory leader then buried his axe in his enemy's skull.

Adair turned back to Mariana. She was trying to walk toward the battlefield.

"No," the prince protested. "You're injured. At least tell me what to do so I can help you."

Mariana shook her head. "I doubt you have the ability to heal."

"I healed Halona. Let me try." Adair frowned stubbornly.

Mariana gave in. She knew his attempts would be futile, but if the boy could muster up the slightest bit of magic, it could work. She carefully began giving Adair instructions on how to focus on bringing the magic into his body. His hand glowed dimly and her eyes widened in surprised. He was healing her!

Mariana smiled at Adair's success. She kept her eyes on the area around them in case someone else attacked. Her eyes widened as she saw an enemy charger toward them with his weapon drawn. As the man approached Mariana, she used what strength she could muster to push Adair to the ground. She threw herself between the prince and a new attacker. The attacker's sword pierced through her stomach. An ear-shattering shriek filled the air as Mariana's body hit the ground.

"Mariana!" Adair hollered as he rushed to grab his sword. He swung at the attacker and plunged his blade through the man's neck. Adair panted as the man's body collapsed to the ground. He took Mariana in his arms. Her eyes were closed.

"No," he said as he put his head on Mariana's chest. He could faintly hear her heartbeat. "Hang on, Mariana," he said as he tried to heal her. Her hand reached up and grasped his. Her eyes opened for a moment. When Adair looked into them, he saw that she was at peace. No words were spoken, but Adair nodded to let her know it was okay to let go. Her eyes closed as Mariana took her final breath.

Chapter 24

Halona and Callahan made it back to the village hours after the fighting ended. Their eyes widened at the carnage they found along the way. Their horror grew when they saw the bodies piling up as they neared the village. Halona scoured the dead, looking for anyone she held dear. She saw familiar faces of her people and she felt sadness that she had not been there to fight alongside them.

"We could have helped," she whispered woefully. "Maybe we would have been able to save a few lives."

Callahan shook his head as his eyes landed on the body of a member of his clan.

"There was nothing we could have done, Halona. It was their time to go. We can only hope they didn't suffer before their lives came to an end."

As Callahan carried Halona through the village, they noticed Evian and Liam carrying people into the medical hut.

"Mariana must be healing the injured." Halona smiled at the thought of returning to her teacher. "She'll need my help."

Callahan nodded and carried the injured girl through the doors to the medical hut. Severin stood in the doorway looking grim. Halona glanced around for her teacher, but she was nowhere to be found. Only Lilith, Callahan's sister, was there healing the injured. Roka and Elias were using their limited knowledge of healing to help whoever they could. Jameson was leaning against a wall to allow his cot to be used.

Halona turned to Severin to ask her question. "Where is Mariana?"

Severin's body tensed and he looked down. This puzzled Halona because she had not seen her serious brother act like this in a long time.

"Severin, where is Mariana?" Halona demanded. She raised her voice which got the attention of many others in the medical hut. Roka's head rose when he heard his daughter. Immediately, he rushed to her side. He pulled her from Callahan's back to bring her into a warm embrace.

"Father?" Her puzzled tone was soft.

Roka held onto his daughter tightly while he spoke with a shaky voice. "The village was attacked by the Itis while you were gone. Mariana was killed in the fight."

Roka felt his heart break as he felt his daughter's body begin to shake. His hand on her back moved in circles. Tears began to spill from Halona's eyes as she wrapped her arms around her father. Her cries became louder and louder as the grief she felt grew more with each passing moment.

Roka stroked his daughter's hair as he had when Elexia had passed. He whispered words to her in the Avory language as she sobbed into his chest.

Chapter 25

dair stared up at the blue sky from his spot by the lake. The guilt from Mariana's death weighed on him heavily. He should have taken her to safety to heal her. He closed his eyes to sink back into his thoughts when he heard footsteps crunching in the grass behind him.

"I thought I might find you here." A soft, familiar voice spoke. Adair did not have to look to know that it was Halona. She was standing behind him, holding herself up on crutches.

"I'm surprised you want to see me," Adair mumbled softly.

"I'm not holding Mariana's death against you, Adair." She sighed as she sat in the grass beside him. "It wasn't your fault."

"She sacrificed her life for mine." Adair opened his eyes. "You should be blaming me. I know I am."

Halona did not meet his gaze. She knew her mentor's death was not Adair's fault, but she could not stop herself from blaming him. Adair could tell that she had been crying. Her face was covered in dried tears and her eyes were puffy with more tears threatening to spill. She pulled her knees to her chest and rested her chin on them.

"Did she suffer?" Halona looked over at the prince.

"What?" Adair raised an eyebrow confused.

"Did she suffer? Did Mariana suffer before she died?"

Adair's eyes softened and he shook his head, "No, she died almost instantly. Her eyes were filled with peace right before she passed."

Halona nodded, "See, I have no reason to hold her death against you. You did not kill her and she did not suffer."

"Are you saying that to convince me or yourself?" Adair asked.

"Both," Halona said as she threw a pebble into the lake.

"Why shouldn't I blame myself?" Adair frowned as he looked out at the water. He threw a pebble into the water and watched the ripples. "I was there. She threw herself between the enemy and my body."

Halona looked at him with tears in her eyes. "I know what you are going through, but eventually you will understand that it was not your fault."

"How the hell do you know what I'm going through?" Adair snapped. "I have lost two people that were dear to me in a matter of months because they sacrificed themselves to save my life. How could you possibly know what I am going through?"

His head snapped in her direction to shoot her glare. Her eyes stayed soft as she looked at him.

"I don't know if you know this, but my mother died protecting me," Halona spoke quietly. "She did not die instantly. She suffered before she passed."

Tears began to spill from Halona's eyes. "She suffered for a long time before she passed away."

Adair looked over at her with regret. He thought back to his conversation with Mariana days before when she had told him about Elexia's death.

"I'm sorry," he said quietly. He was sure Halona had not heard him, but he did not notice the small smile on her lips. She leaned over and took his hand in hers as she laid her head on his shoulder.

"When the people we care about are gone," Halona whispered, her voice cracking. "We can't do anything but honor their memory and they life they had."

Adair glanced at her from the corner of his eye. He nodded and gave her hand a small squeeze as he watched her close her eyes as the sun began to set.

Chapter 26

Roka stood over the beaten man. The Avory leader's eyes were filled with fury. The man before him was tied to a chair with his arms painfully bent behind his back.

"Who sent you too attack us?" Roka demanded. "Your clan has not come close to our borders in years."

"I don't gotta tell you nothing." The man spit at the Avory leader's feet. Roka brought up a fist and in one swoop, he punched the man in the stomach.

The injured man coughed and blood dripped from the man's lip. Roka brought up his fist again and landed another punch. Again, the man coughed up blood.

"A'ight, a'ight! I'll tell ya," the man begged, nearly incoherent from his injuries. "We're workin' with the Ivane."

Roka stepped forward, causing the man to flinch. The leader grabbed ahold of the man's collar and pulled him forward.

"What are the Ivane planning?"

"I heard that they and Uron is workin' t'gether," he said, stumbling with his words.

"Uron." Roka looked at the man, surprised. "The country?"

The man nodded. "Ya, ya! The country. They's tryin' to start a war."

Roka stood up straight and turned to one of the guards positioned at the door. "Kill him. I have all the information that I need."

The guard nodded as his leader exited the room. Shouts could be heard coming from the man as the guard stepped closer to him. Eventually, after several minutes of shouting, the room fell silent.

Roka returned to the meeting room where Elias, Callahan, and Liam were waiting. Roka relayed the information from the interrogation.

"What is your plan, Roka?" The old man looked at his friend with concern. "If the Ivane have enough of an influence to have a clan from the east attack us, then we could be attacked from the north as well."

"I know. We need to be ready in case another clan decides to attack. I am sending Halona and Adair to the Arian capital. We need King Roland on our side for this war. If Uron is trying to take over, I'm sure he is aware of the upcoming threats. He may already be preparing Aria for war. Aligning with Aria may be our only chance. We don't know the numbers of the Ivane army. We'll need as many soldiers as possible."

Elias nodded slowly and glanced at his son. "I will send Callahan with them. We will ally ourselves with Aria as well."

Roka sighed as he sat in a large chair in his meeting room. "We can only pray that the prophecy will happen. We must hope that our Peace Bringers will be successful. I don't like the idea of sending my daughter into Arian territory, but as a Peace Bringer, it is her destiny."

Chapter 27

King Roland frowned as he stared out at the setting sun from his bedroom balcony. The grave news that he received from King Olric from Etras—that Etrasian villages were being attacked daily by savages and Uronian armies were taking the conquered territory— did not help ease his troubled mind. The bad news continued to pile on.

"Sir, we have reason to believe that savage tribes are being attacked by a nomadic savage clan." One of his advisors spoke softly at their nightly meeting hours before.

"Attacked?" King Roland frowned. "Are you positive?"

"No, but we have sources that informed us of a traveling clan passing by several villages. This clan is usually known to attack the villages that it passes through. They were last spotted to the west of the capital, but they never returned the way they came. They disappeared."

King Roland ran a hand through his beard.

"Maybe the Avory stopped their attack," the king suggested aloud. "Or maybe there was no attack at all."

Another advisor spoke. "The clan was seen with weapons. We believe they were headed to attack something. Perhaps Eyra knows something."

King Roland nodded and dismissed his advisors before paying a visit to Eyra in his jail cell. Their conversation had been short.

"Uron will be at our border soon," Eyra spoke. "As for the savage army, they have been dealt with."

"And what of my son?"

Eyra smiled. "Adair is safe and well among the Avory, but he will be returning very soon."

King Roland narrowed his eyes at the old man. "For your sake, you better be right."

King Roland turned on his heels and left Eyra in his prison cell. He headed for his bed chambers. His wife was still bedridden and ill. Dark circles surrounded her eyes and her skin looked sickly. Roland sat at the foot of their bed and placed a hand on her knee.

"Eyra says that Adair is safe and should be returning to us soon."

Abry's eyes opened and she looked at him, trying to sit up to talk to her husband. "Do you believe his words?"

King Roland sighed. "I do not know, but I do hope that he speaks the truth. Unfortunately, he also believes that we may soon be at war."

"Let us hope that everything will play out in the end," she said from the bed. "Adair is a Peace Bringer. If a war is about to start, he will end it."

"I do hope you are right, my love."

Chapter 28

dair sighed as a pink petal fell from his head and into his lap. He watched, curious and slightly irritated, as Halona weaved flowers into a crown for herself. She had already adorned Adair with a crown made from the pink flowers nearby. She had placed it on his head so gently that he had almost missed the fact that she was doing it. It was only when she sneezed that he knew she was behind him.

"Do I have to wear this stupid thing?"

"Yes," she said, putting the final touches on her crown. She placed it on her head and grinned.

"You look ridiculous."

Halona said nothing, but she continued to smile as she started to make more crowns. She handed a bundle of flowers to Adair.

"No."

She added a handful of daisies to the pink pile.

"I am not helping you make flower crowns for your brothers."

"Who said that these were for my brothers?" She asked. "What if I want to make one for my father."

Adair blinked as he tried to imagine Roka wearing a flower crown made from cherry blossoms during combat. He chuckled to himself as he imagined Halona also decorating her father's armor with daisies.

"That would be interesting," he said.

Halona laughed as she placed a second finished crown on her head. "Well, I doubt he'd wear it anyway, which is why I have you. I mean, you still have to do everything I say."

Adair chuckled. "I bet your brothers would wear one."

"Oh definitely. I have those idiots wrapped around my finger."

Time passed and Halona finished more crowns, creating a pile of them on her and Adair's heads. When her hands began to cramp after she had completed about ten crowns, she lay back in the grass and began to look up at the clouds.

"That one looks like a rabbit," she said, pointing to the sky. The cloud did indeed look like a rabbit with what Adair pictured were floppy ears and a bushy tail.

"That one looks like a sword," Adair said. The cloud he pointed to was almost straight and to him looked like it had a handle.

"Nah, that is stick."

Adair sat up and glanced at her. "Where is your imagination?"

Halona pointed to the sky near the sword cloud. "The cloud next to it looks like a tree, so that cloud must be a stick that fell from the tree."

Adair shook his head and laughed to himself.

The two continued to cloud gaze until the sun had begun to set. Adair reached toward the sky to point out a cloud that he thought looked like Roka when he noticed that Halona had fallen asleep beside him. He thought about waking her so that they could head back to the village, but he decided against it. He stood and stretched his legs and arms out before reaching down to pick her up. She stirred lightly in his arms, but otherwise stayed asleep.

A deep laugh sounded from behind him and he turned to see Severin walking toward him. It was one of the few times that Adair had heard the man make any sort of humored noise.

"I'll grab her crutches. Let's talk and walk," Severin said. He picked up Halona's crutches and held them over his shoulder as he led the way back to the village.

"Father is sending you back to Arian territory," Severin said.

"What why?" Adair said. "Don't get me wrong, that is great news. It is just a little sudden and unexpected from your father."

Severin nodded. "With the recent attack on the village and the information gained from the interrogation of enemy survivors, my father and Elias both believe that an alliance with your father is our best chance at winning this upcoming war."

"You think my father would accept an alliance offer with your people? My people believe you all to be savages, and while my views have changed, my father's opinion may not. Especially since I have essentially been held captive here for months."

Severin nodded. "Yes, which is why he is also sending my sister, Callahan, Evian, and myself with you. Callahan is meant to form the alliance between Aria and his clan. You, Halona, and I are meant to form the alliance between my clan and Aria. Evian is going because he needs to stay out of trouble."

"Halona's ankle has not healed yet," Adair argued. "Traveling on it won't be good for her."

"She'll be fine. She has dealt with worse than a broken ankle and survived."

Adair nodded, unsure, but not willing to argue further with Severin. He adjusted Halona in his arms and they were soon at the entrance to the village. Two guards posted at the entrance bowed to Severin before letting the two men pass.

As they passed the medical hut, Adair imagined Mariana closing it up for the night. He imagined her coming up to him and handing him a cup for Halona to drink that would relieve her of the pain in her ankle. As she turned away from him, she smiled and waved. He smiled and waved back before realizing that it was an illusion. He cleared his throat and coughed to choke back the lump growing in his throat.

Halona woke and glanced up at Adair and followed his gaze to the medical hut. She took in a deep breath and swallowed the lump in her throat before pretending to go back to sleep. When they reached their home and Adair had laid Halona in her bed, she silently cried herself back to sleep.

Roka woke her the next morning to inform her of her mission. She nodded and got out of bed. Her hair stuck to her face in a mixture of sweat and tears from the night before. While she dressed herself and packed, Adair waited in the main room.

"I hope you understand how important this is," Roka said to Adair as he left Halona's room.

Adair nodded. "I do, and thank you."

"Don't thank me. I am doing what I need to do to protect my people. I do not want this war to be against Aria as well. When she is dressed, I want you both to meet the others at the village entrance," he said before walking out of the house.

Adair sighed and ran a hand through his hair. He had been dreaming of going home since he arrived, but now it felt bittersweet. He looked at the flower crowns sitting in a pile on one of the chairs and smiled. He reached out to pick one up and held it for a while. When he heard the door to Halona's room open, he turned around and laughed.

Halona wore her normal garb, but her hair was sticking up in multiple places. She was attempting to braid it and failing.

"Don't laugh at me!" she said with a frown as she opted to pull her hair into a messy bun instead of braiding it.

"I wasn't laughing at you," Adair said.

"Really?" She put her hands on her hips. "Because no one else was laughing for you to laugh with."

Adair cleared his throat and gently placed the flower crown on her head. "It will hide how bad your hair looks."

She frowned and gave him a playful glare before grabbing a flower crown. She stood on her toes to set it on his head. She put the crown on crooked and it leaned to one side.

Adair chuckled to himself. "What is that supposed to hide?"

Halona smirked. "Your big head." She left the house before he could respond. She began running once she made it to the road. Her injured ankle kept her from running too fast.

Adair followed her, laughing to himself. He ran slower to give her the illusion that she was winning their race. He caught up to her just as she reached the village entrance.

"I won!" She grinned.

"I didn't know we were racing," Adair said with a grin, crossing his arms. "Otherwise, I would have beaten you."

Halona laughed and shrugged. She sat down on a large rock. She motioned for Adair to join her by the rock and he did, standing off to the side of it. She pulled a small knife from her boot and began to carve her name into the stone.

"Are you excited to see your family again?" she asked without looking up from the rock.

Adair gave her a small nod. "Yes, but it will be strange. I've been gone for so long."

"I'm sure that they'll be happy to see you," she smiled.

He nodded.

Maybe seeing his parents was the thing he needed to help him come to terms with Mariana's death. Halona seemed to be taking it well, and he found it strange.

"Can I ask you something?" He looked at her curiously before looking around to see if anyone was watching him.

She nodded, "Go ahead."

"How have you been so calm about Mariana's death?"

Halona closed her eyes and paused for a moment before opening them again. She shook her head. "I haven't been as calm as you think. Every night for the past several days, I have been crying myself to sleep."

He opened his mouth to respond, but closed it when Severin, Callahan, and Evian came into view. Each of the three men were holding their own pack of supplies and weapons.

"Father is sending you with us?" Halona looked at them surprised.

Callahan shrugged. "My father is sending me. If the Avory are going to align themselves with Aria, then the Orasi should as well. It's beneficial to everyone involved."

She nodded and turned to her brothers for clarification on their sudden appearance.

"You seriously think father would send you to the capital of Aria with only Adair?" Evian laughed. "He isn't that trusting."

Adair frowned and glared at Evian. "I have done nothing to cause him to distrust me!"

"Father knows you're our ally now. It's only that he doesn't want our precious baby sister to go on a journey with a man she barely knows. Too many bad things could happen." Evian shrugged.

Severin nodded in agreement. "We aren't taking the risk."

Adair's eyes widened, "You think that I would take advantage of Halona?"

Severin and Evian exchanged a glance before replying in unison. "Yes."

Adair's mouth hung open in disbelief, and Halona rolled her eyes before glancing toward the forest. The bodies had been cleared and the forest held no evidence that a battle had occurred.

"I trust you five will have a safe journey," Roka said from behind them.

She turned to face him with a smile. "Of course. We'll return safe and with a signed treaty."

Roka nodded. "I've entrusted the signing to Callahan and Severin. I would send Liam, but since he is my heir, I need him here with me."

"Then why does Callahan have to come?" Halona whined. "He's Elias's heir."

"I'm going *because* I am my father's heir," Callahan scoffed. "He trusts me to be an ambassador for our clan for this task."

Roka nodded in agreement as he extended his hand to give Severin a piece of parchment. Severin look it and gently placed it in his pack.

Roka patted his sons on the back and bid them farewell before bringing his daughter into a warm embrace. "Be careful, Halona," he said quietly as he kissed the top of her head.

"I'll be fine, Father," she said with a sigh. "I have plenty of protectors." Her eyes fell on the men that were going to journey with her.

Roka nodded as he released his daughter. "Go, you have a long journey ahead of you."

She nodded in return and gave her father a quick kiss on the cheek. They all knew they journey would take them days without horses. If the horses were not all needed to prepare for the upcoming battle, they could cut their travel time down to only a day.

"Let's go." Severin's deep voice boomed through the forest. He was not talking loudly, but his voice usually carried far. The others nodded and began following him as he led the way through the forest to the edge of the Avory territory.

Chapter 29

dair stared into the flames of the fire burning before him. The group had journeyed long into the night. Halona's injured ankle had begun to give her trouble around sunset. They decided to continue walking as long as they could in the dark, staying on guard for any threats lurking within the shadows.

"We should continue walking into the night," Severin suggested. "Are you okay to continue, Halona?"

Halona nodded, trying to hide her pain from the others. "Yeah, I can go a bit longer."

"Are you sure?" Adair asked. "I noticed that you've been limping for quite a while."

Evian nodded. "I caught that too. Maybe we should stop."

Callahan scoffed. "If she says she's fine then she's fine."

"We don't want her slowing us down and we don't want her to permanently damage her ankle," Severin said. "We're stopping for the night. This place seems as good as any."

"Severin, I'm fine, really," Halona protested.

Severin raised an eyebrow as he picked up a stick. He tapped Halona's injured ankle with it, sending her to the ground.

"Ow!" She hissed. "What was that for?"

"To show you that you aren't fine. Your ankle is clearly bothering you."

Halona grumbled as she began to dig around in her pack. She pulled out a small, leather bag labeled "pain relief," a bowl, and an herb grinder. She took out some herbs from the bag and grinded them into a paste, then added water to the bowl. The putrid smell of the herbs and water filled the air. She put the bowl to her lips and took a long drink, coughing once she finished.

"Keep an eye on me," she said. "It's possible this stuff will make me vomit."

"Ew," Evian said. "Then why are you drinking it?"

"Because it will numb the pain in my ankle, Moron."

"How is your ankle?" Severin asked as he inspected his sister's foot.

"It's fine. I'm sure I'll be able to walk in the morning," she huffed. "Those herbs that I drank should at least work through the night to let me get some rest. I can drink what is left in the morning so that I don't slow us down. Unless you all decide you need to be manly men and carry the damsel in distress."

"Cut the sass," Evian scolded. You should have told us that it was bothering you. We could have stopped earlier."

"If she hadn't of gotten us lost during the hunt, her ankle wouldn't be injured," Callahan accused. He was sitting against a tree away from the others as he polished his sword with a rag.

Halona shot him a glare, "Watch it, pretty boy. My shoulder is fine. I can still shoot you with an arrow and don't think that I won't do it!" She pointed her finger at him.

Callahan said nothing as he rolled his eyes before going back to polishing his weapon.

While Halona was arguing with her brothers and Callahan, Adair took everyone's cloaks and folded them into a pile to elevate Halona's foot. When he was done, he sat against a tree not far from her.

Severin gently sat Halona's foot on the stack of cloaks. "Get some rest and don't vomit," he said.

"I'll try," she said, giving him a thumbs-up. Soon after, she found herself rushing to the bushes to expel the contents of her stomach. When she was finished, she sat back down and returned her foot to the stack of clothes.

"How are you feeling?" she said asked Adair.

"I'm alright," he said with a shrug. They both knew it was not true, but it was the best they could hope for.

"We should all get some rest," Evian spoke up. "I'll take first watch."

"I'll do it," Adair offered.

Evian glanced over at the man and raised an eyebrow. "You sure?"

Adair only nodded in response.

"Alright, wake me up when you get tired." Evian laid down in his sleeping bag and quickly began to snore. Everyone soon followed into their own dreams.

Adair kept his focus on the forest. He kept his sword nearby as he watched for any sign of danger. An hour had passed when he began to hear whimpering. His gaze searched through the small portion of the forest that he could see. The whimper seemed almost human. It took him several minutes to realize that it was Halona who was making the sound.

She seemed to be shaking in her sleeping bag. Her face was contorted in pain as she slept. Adair looked down at the girl's sleeping form and gently shook her shoulder.

"Halona," he whispered. She did not wake up. He shook her and whispered again. This time her eyes shot open quickly as she looked around.

"Are you alright?" Adair looked down at her, concerned. Her eyes were beginning to swell with tears. She nodded, but he could easily tell she was lying.

"It was just a bad dream," she mumbled. She lay back down in her bag before closing her eyes. She could not go back to sleep no matter how hard she tried.

"Adair?" she whispered innocently.

"Hmm?" He glanced over at her.

"Could I lay beside you?" Her face flushed. Adair chuckled softly at her embarrassed expression and extended a hand.

"Come here."

Halona smiled as she crawled over and lay down close to him. His hand found its way into her hair where it gently stroked her red locks until she fell asleep.

Evian awoke not long after and smirked at the sight of his sister and the prince.

"I'm watching you, Adair," he said, and raised an eyebrow and pointed to the prince's hands. "Keep your hands to yourself."

"Goodnight," Adair said and laughed as he leaned his head back against the tree.

◇•◇•◇

Halona's eyes fluttered opened the next morning. She felt something tangled in her hair. Her eyes glanced upward to see Adair lying next to her against the tree and his hand was resting on her head.

Her eyes glanced to the side where she saw Severin preparing breakfast. There were a few fish speared and cooking over the fire along with an unidentifiable meat. She yawned as she debated waking up or staying on the ground a little longer.

She made her decision when she felt Adair begin to stir. His hand came out of her hair as he stretched his arms. She closed her eyes and pretended to sleep for a while longer.

"Will someone wake her lazy ass," Callahan stated. "We don't have time to waste."

"Calm down, Callahan." Evian laughed. "You're just grumpy because she chose Adair and not you."

Adair's head snapped in their direction at the mention of his name.

Callahan cringed. "I would be attracted to a bear before I was attracted to her. Let the stupid prince have her."

Halona figured now was as good a time as any to wake up because it was easier to respond to Callahan's insults than to ignore them. She sat up and shot the Orasi heir a glare before rolling up her sleeping bag and putting it away.

"At least I don't suck my thumb in my sleep," she said.

Evian snickered and added, "Like a little baby."

"Will you three knock it off and eat," Severin scolded.

He passed Halona a stick with rabbit meat on it and she thanked him. Severin then passed the food out to everyone else.

"We all need to get along," he lectured. "I doubt King Roland will take any of us seriously if we argue the entire trip."

Adair nodded in agreement. "If Father sees that you can't get along as allies, he won't trust you to be his."

Adair stood and stretched again as he began to eat his speared fish. He cringed at the pungent flavor as it hit his taste buds. Halona was the only one who seemed to notice and she laughed softly. Adair heard the soft sound and shot her a glare which only caused her to laugh more.

"We'll head back out when everyone finishes eating." Evian said, and tossed the spear that his fish had been on into the fire. He had devoured the food in a matter of seconds.

Adair sighed as he tried to eat the rest of the disgusting fish. He knew he needed to eat, but it was so foul that it made him want to vomit. He heard a sigh from beside him and saw Halona extending the spear that her meat was on.

"I'll trade you," she smiled. "This is rabbit meat."

"Thanks," Adair laughed as he took the rabbit in exchange for the fish. He bit into the soft flesh and sighed again. This time it was a content sigh. The rabbit meat was nowhere near as awful as the fish had been. He watched in horror as Halona finished the rest of the fish. She made no sign of disgust and he wondered if the woman had taste buds at all.

Once everyone was finished eating, Severin put out the fire and the group was off once more. They still had several more days of traveling before they reached the Arian capital.

fter traveling for several more hours, Adair noticed Halona falling behind. She was trying her best to keep up, but it seemed that her injured ankle was still bothering her. He fell behind to keep her company.

"How's your ankle doing?" He looked down at it concerned. She was limping and he could tell she was trying to hide the pain.

"Fine," she lied.

"Halona," he gave her a stern look.

"What are you, my brother?" She rolled her eyes. "I said it is fine."

"You're limping. It is obviously bothering you," he argued. He continued to stare at her until she gave in.

She sighed with a nod, giving in, "It's still bothering me."

"Will you be able to walk on it much longer?"

She shrugged. "I don't know, but I can try."

Adair shook his head and took the pack off his back. He walked up to Evian before whispering something that Halona could not hear. Evian nodded and took Adair's pack from him. Adair returned to Halona's side and in a split second was carrying her.

Halona squeaked in surprise, "What are you doing? Put me down!" She wiggled and squirmed.

"You're going to slow us down if you continue to limp. I'm going to carry you for a little while." He spoke like it was an insult, but Halona could hear a slight tinge of concern in his voice.

"Fine," she huffed and wrapped her arms around his neck while he carried her on his back. "But don't drop me."

As if to test his boundaries, Adair pretended to drop and catch her. She yelled at him and lectured him for several minutes.

At the front of the group, Evian smirked at his older brother. "Are you thinking what I'm thinking?"

Severin nodded with a frown. "Yes, and I don't like it."

Adair continued with Halona on his back until the sun set. Severin decided the group was close enough to the Avory border that they could rest early for the night without losing time. With Adair carrying Halona, their speed had increased.

Adair carefully set Halona on the ground by the fire. The autumn air was getting chillier as the night went on. He wrapped his cloak around her shoulders and sat beside her.

"Halona, can I tell you something?" he asked.

She smiled and nodded. "Sure, we're friends. You can tell me anything."

The term "friends" hit Adair hard in the chest. She only thought they were friends. There was nothing more? Doubts and worries began flooding his head as he thought about what rejection would feel like.

He shook his head and gave her a smile. "Never mind, it was stupid."

"You sure?" She tilted her head to the side, confused.

"Yeah."

Halona shrugged and brushed off the situation as she laid out her sleeping bag. Callahan took first watch and, although she would hate to put her life in his hands in any other situation, she knew that he was not stupid enough to get them all killed. He had to keep up the alliance and with three dead Avory and a dead Arian prince, his chances of doing just that would be slim.

Evian and Severin lay down in their own sleeping bags with their weapons close by. It was clear that they did not trust Callahan, but they also knew that he would not jeopardize his clan.

Halona quickly fell asleep close to Adair's side. For a moment, he raised his hand to run it through her hair again, but her words echoed through his head. His mind began playing tricks on him as he began to think of situations that had not even happened.

"We're friends. Nothing more."

"I don't think you are suitable for me."

"You have feelings for me? That's ridiculous!"

These thoughts continued throughout the night and turned into his nightmares. On top of the rejection, he continued to feel guilty for Mariana's death.

In sleep, Adair's body returned to the forest. The dead bodies of his fallen comrades, both Arian and Avory, lay around him in a large pile. On the top of that pile rested Mariana's body. Slowly, the bodies began to move and stand as they took steps closer to Adair.

He did not run this time. Instead, he stood still and let their hands claw at his flesh.

"You killed us!" they chanted. "You let us die!"

Two bodies stood at the front of the mob. One was Bennett and the other Mariana.

"You could have saved us, you fool!" Mariana's low voice had been replaced with a deep growl.

"You could have saved us!" Bennett's dead body echoed with the same low growl.

"I'm sorry," Adair whispered. "Kill me then. Kill me now."

Just as Bennett brought his sword up to bring it down into Adair's skull, a flash of red hair caught Adair's eye. Before he knew it, he was being dragged away by a redhaired woman. It had to be Halona. She was saving him, but why?

"Halona," he whispered once they were safe. "You should have left me back there to die. I deserve it."

She turned around and Adair's eyes widened. This woman was not Halona. She was similar in many aspects, but her facial features were more defined. She had the same red hair, pale skin, green eyes, and freckles, but this woman was not the girl he had grown to know.

"Who are you?" Adair asked.

"Why, Adair, you should know," she spoke. Her voice was calm and silvery.

"No, I don't." Adair stared at her. "I'm sorry."

"But I look like someone you know," she said with a smile. "My daughter, perhaps?"

Adair's eyes widened. This was Halona's mother?

"I am Elexia." She answered his unasked question and smiled warmly.

"What are you doing here?" Adair glanced around, looking for any sign of the zombies nearby.

"I am here to give you advice." She brushed a strand of hair from his eyes. "Halona has taken a liking to you, and you to her. I can't be there for her anymore physically, so I can only hope to provide for her through the spirit world."

"Spirit world?" Adair's eyebrow raised.

Elexia nodded, "Those who have found favor with the Moon or Polaris are given the opportunity to speak with the dead."

"Then why were Bennett and Mariana chasing me?" He looked at her skeptically.

"Your mind is not ready to see their spirits, but it will be in time. When the time comes, they will appear to you. The Moon asked me to bring a message to you."

Adair again looked skeptical. He still did not believe in the Moon Spirit or Fate.

Elexia continued. "You must be careful. Tragedy will befall you again and there are two ways that you could go. You could continue the path of a Peace Bringer and end the war, or you will succumb to your grief and perish. It all depends on the choices you make."

"What does this have to do with your daughter?" Adair leaned his back against a tree. Something about Elexia put his mind at ease.

"Halona will also have to make a split-second decision. She may appear fine on the outside, but within she is suffering from Mariana's death. She has the same two paths that she could take. I am entrusting you with keeping her on the right path. You two are destined to do great things together."

Adair opened his mouth to speak again, but Elexia disappeared in a flash of light. The bright light enveloped Adair and soon he was dropped into darkness.

Adair's eyes fluttered open. The sun was only just beginning to rise. Severin was awake and keeping watch. Halona slept close to Adair's side. She was breathing softly as she clutched the cloak around her shoulders in her fist.

Adair looked around at the others. Severin was nowhere to be found and Callahan was resting. Evian was throwing more logs onto the fire. He caught Adair's gaze and gave him a small wave. Adair waved back.

He heard mumbling beside him and felt something touch him. He looked down at Halona who was now laying closer to him.

Her head was beside his chest. He brought his hand down to gently tap her shoulder.

Her eyes slowly opened as she yawned. "Is it morning yet?"

Adair chuckled and laughed. "Yeah, it is."

She nodded sleepily and sat up. Adair had to stifle a laugh when he saw the twig poking from her head. He reached over and gently pulled it from the mess of red hair.

"Thanks," she said with a blush.

He nodded and began to stand and pack his things back into his travel pack. Severin soon returned with several rabbits and fish. He skinned and gutted them before spearing the meat onto sticks and roasting them over the fire.

Adair watched as Halona stretched and packed her things. He debated about telling her about his dream last night, but decided to wait.

"How far from the border are we?" He looked over at her. He pulled out his sword to clean the blade.

"We'll reach the border sometime today. After that, we'll have to be more careful about traveling. Who knows who we will encounter."

Adair nodded and glanced toward the fire. "I'm surprised we haven't found anyone yet."

Halona laughed. "Not many people are stupid enough to enter our territory. After all, we have that fence of heads at the border."

Adair raised his eyebrow. "I thought those were just rotting fruit."

Halona nodded. "They were, but only because we had not seen battle in so long. Since the battle with the Itis, scouts are replacing the fruit with real heads."

Her voice cracked when she mentioned the battle.

Adair cringed with a sigh before sitting by the fire. The others soon joined him as Severin passed around breakfast before dousing the fire.

"Let's go, we should get an early start today." Adair stood with his stick of food. "We can eat along the way."

Everyone nodded at their unofficial leader. Adair turned to Halona to ask about her ankle.

She waved him off and smiled. "I can walk on my own today. My ankle is feeling better."

He nodded and the two followed behind the others as they traveled.

Chapter 30

"King Roland, Sir!" A guard rushed into the throne room of the Arian king. The king looked unamused by the guard's rude entrance, but let the man speak.

The man bowed several times before panting. He had run all the way from the western gates of the capital. "Prince Adair has returned to us!" he said.

King Roland stood and began bombarding the young gate guard with questions.

"Adair is here? Are you certain? How do you know it was my son? Is he well? Is he injured? Where is he now?" King Roland stepped toward the guard and grabbed him by the shoulders and shook him.

"He entered through the western gates with a group of savages," the guard explained. "They are being escorted here as we speak."

King Roland nodded and sent more guards to receive the group. King Roland sat on his throne shaking his leg impatiently while he waited. He sent a servant to retrieve his wife from the gardens. She had begun to recover slowly and could now move about once more.

Queen Abry arrived with a joyous expression. "My love, is it true? Has our Adair really returned?" She threw her arms around her husband happily.

King Roland nodded. "He is on his way. He has been traveling with a band of savages."

Queen Abry gasped and nodded. "The letter he sent us must have been genuine then."

King Roland nodded. "I have no more doubts that it was not from him, however, I am concerned that he has returned with a group of savages."

Abry spoke. "What do they want?"

"I do not know, but as long as Adair is alive and well, I do not care. Once he is here, he will be returned to us and I will have that entire clan executed, starting with the savages he led here."

Queen Abry nodded. "Yes, of course. We need Adair more than ever now."

King Roland nodded, covering his mouth as he began to cough. "Yes, my love. We do."

Chapter 31

dair took in a deep breath as he walked through the familiar halls of the palace. The strange thing was that this place had been his home for twenty years, but it did not feel like home.

Halona stayed close to Adair. When they entered through the gates of the capital, they had been met with swords. Adair had to assure the guards that his travel companions meant no harm. He warned Halona to stay close to him for her own safety.

Halona walked beside Adair with her bow clutched tightly in her hands, her knuckles were turning white. This palace was larger than any building or village that she had ever been in. She felt Adair's hand on her shoulder. She turned and saw him giving her a reassuring smile. It did not help much, but her nerves settled slightly.

Adair took another breath when their escorts stopped in front of the throne room. He glanced at his traveling party. They were all on edge. The guards surrounding them were not hiding the fact that the savages were not welcome. The men were pointing swords at the group.

The large doors to the throne room opened. As soon as the group stepped through the doors, Queen Abry jumped from her throne and rushed toward them.

"My son!" she cried as she pulled Adair into her arms. She held him close to her chest. Adair stared in shock and carefully hugged his mother back.

"Hello, Mother," he said with a soft laugh.

Queen Abry pulled away to get a good look at him. To her surprise, he was not in terrible shape. He was not skinnier than he should have been. His brown hair was much longer than she remembered, and he also sported thick dark stubble on his chin. There were two things that caused her mother's heart concern. The first was that his usually bright eyes appeared dull and tired. The second was the small, savage woman that seemed to be clinging to his side.

Queen Abry stepped away from her son and turned to Halona. She inspected the girl under a hard gaze. Her eyes narrowed and her mouth twisted into a frown. Adair had never seen such a look on his mother's face.

Halona, out of both fear and respect, curtsied to the Arian Queen, but the girl made no sound.

"Who are you?" Queen Abry demanded, staring down at the small redhead.

Severin's protectiveness began to show as he took a step toward his sister and the queen. Guards immediately raised their weapons.

Adair threw his hands in the air to stop the guards from attacking his traveling party.

"Stop. They're friends of mine." Adair pushed himself between the others and the guards. The guards lowered their weapons, but kept their grips on the handles.

"Mother." Adair turned to Queen Abry. "I would like you to meet my friend, Princess Halona of the Avory Clan. She and her family have shown me great hospitality. I mentioned her in my letter."

Queen Abry's eyes widened. "Were you forced to write that letter?"

Adair shook his head. "No. Roka, the Avory leader, asked me to write it so that you and Father would know that I was alive. We were worried that Father would send another army."

"What happened to my army?" King Roland asked.

"A storm blew through the area causing a lot of destruction," Adair spoke. "The army ended up being in the center of it all, and we only found one survivor. He is currently in recovery back in the Avory village."

King Roland stood from his throne and strutted over to the group. He stood tall with his shoulders back. He stopped in front of Adair with a hard look in his eyes.

"Father," Adair said, and nodded in respect.

Without warning, King Roland grabbed his son by the shoulders and brought him forward in an embrace. "Welcome home, Adair."

Adair smiled and returned his father's embrace. Halona could not help but smile at the reunion.

When the family was done reuniting, King Roland turned to the group before him. "Why were you sent here with my son? Give me one good reason why I shouldn't execute you all right now."

Severin stepped forward and gave a short bow. Callahan did as well.

"I am Severin, the son of the Avory leader, Roka. My father sent me to ask for an alliance for an upcoming war that we believe your country and our clans will be dragged into."

"I assume you are having problems as well?" King Roland returned to his throne and gestured for the guards to bring the savages closer.

Severin nodded. "A couple of weeks ago, our village was attacked by a nomadic clan. We have learned from prisoners that the Ivane, a large clan located within the borders of Uron, is taking territory from other clans in Etras. We suspect that Uronian armies are following and claiming that territory for Uron. It is only a matter of time before they pass the Arian border and take territory belonging to you and our clans."

King Roland rested his chin on his fist. "I heard about the attack. We had news that a traveling clan was passing by villages instead of attacking them. If what you say about Uron is true, then it will not be long before the Uronian army is at Aria's eastern border."

Severin nodded and gestured to Callahan. "As I'm sure you are aware, the Orasi clan's territory is on the border between your country and Etras. Callahan is the heir to the Orasi clan. The Orasi and Avory have been allies for centuries. Both clans are looking to form an alliance with Aria to stop what threatens all of our people. By aligning with us, your northern border would be protected against the Ivane and their allies. We could prevent them from crossing the border and attacking your villages by sending warriors up there to defend it."

Adair stepped up to add to Severin's explanation. "Halona is the other Peace Bringer," he said, gesturing toward the girl.

King Roland's eyes widened before he belted out a hearty laugh. "Her? That weak looking girl is the other Peace Bringer?"

Halona frowned and took a step forward. She held her bow in her hand, but no arrow. Confidence and anger replaced her fear and worry.

"I assure you, Your Majesty, that I am not weak. If you would allow me, I would like to prove it," she challenged.

King Roland laughed again. "Go ahead, girl."

The King called in several servants. He had apples placed on each of their heads.

King Roland stood and walked toward Halona. He leaned into her face, intimidating her with his size.

"Shoot the apples off these servants. If you can shoot all of them, Aria will form an alliance with your savage clans," the king ordered as the men lined up against a back wall. He returned to his seat and leaned forward, ready to watch her fail.

Halona nocked an arrow and held up her bow. It did not take long for her to fire once. The tip of the arrow went through the center of the first apple and lodged in the wall. She rapidly fired another arrow. It hit its target. Instead of firing a third arrow, she smirked. She reached into her boot to retrieve a small knife. She threw it at the final apple and sliced it in half. She retrieved the knife, returning it to her boot before placing her bow on her back. She mockingly curtsied to the king.

"Unlike your armies, we have women warriors. Men and women are equals on the battle field," she lectured.

King Roland sat on his throne in shock. No words came from his mouth. Adair flashed Halona a proud smile which she returned.

"Aria will align with your clans," King Roland managed to sputter. Halona grinned as she and Evian exchanged a secret high-five.

"But, you will return Aria's heir to us," the king continued.

Adair looked at Halona. She seemed sad, almost as if she knew that his would be his answer.

"Father, I'm afraid that may not be possible," Adair spoke up. Halona glanced over at him, surprised.

"Why not?" King Roland frowned. Everyone else in the room seemed to be surprised as well.

"How will we be able to offer aid on the battlefield if we have no one there to command our armies? I propose that you allow me to lead the division you send to help the clans fight. I have been with the Avory for quite some time. They would be more likely to trust me than one of your generals." Adair stood tall as he addressed his father.

King Roland seemed to be taken aback by his son's straightforwardness. "Are you certain that this is what you want, Adair?"

Adair nodded. "I am indebted to the Avory for saving my life and to Halona for nursing me back to health when I was injured. I wish to stay with them and command the Arian forces as they fight alongside the Avory and Orasi."

King Roland mulled over the idea for several minutes. Finally, he answered. "Very well. I will send two thousand soldiers with you to command."

Adair grinned. He had not expected his idea to work, but it had. He turned to Halona and picked her up in an excited embrace before putting her down. Afterward, both their faces flushed at the spectacle.

King Roland cleared his throat to return order to his throne room. "Uron has been advancing toward our eastern border. I will be heading there to lead the main armies."

Adair nodded. "Of course, Father."

With nothing more to discuss, the treaty was signed, signaling the end of the meeting.

When the meeting was over, King Roland had two thousand men assembled to send back with Adair and his band of savages. They had orders to obey their prince under any circumstance. This war was happening and it was happening fast.

Chapter 32

Roka stood in his chamber with Halona, Severin, Evian, and Callahan. They had returned from their journey that morning.

Severin placed the signed treaty into his father's hand. Roka unraveled the paper and scanned the document, making sure all the necessary signatures were there. Once he checked it over, he rolled it back up and turned to Halona.

"Go see how Adair and Liam are doing with the armies. We will be heading out at dawn tomorrow and they need to be ready," Roka ordered.

Halona nodded before rushing out to find her brother and Adair. She found them on the training grounds. Tents had been set up around the village for the two thousand men that King Roland sent back with them.

Adair noticed Halona as he was helping a younger man on his sword techniques. He smiled and waved to her as she approached.

"Father sent me to check on things. We're leaving tomorrow." She glanced around at the soldiers training. Some of the Avory warriors were helping the Arian soldiers learn the tactics of savage warfare.

Adair nodded. "Our foot soldiers are doing fine and my men are picking up the new style of fighting easily, but we're going to need someone to lead our archers."

Halona caught Adair's hint and she stared at him wide-eyed. "You want me to lead them?"

Adair nodded. "You're the best archer that I know. Who else could do it?"

Halona shook her head. "I'm not a leader."

Adair placed his hands on her shoulders. "Please, Halona. You're the only person that Liam and I would feel comfortable entrusting to lead them. Your father talked to us about it as well."

Halona sighed. "Okay, but will your men listen to me?"

"They will if it is an order. You may be a woman, but if I respect you, they will as well." Adair gave her a small smile which she returned.

"I'll do it," she said with a sigh. Adair grinned and gave her a small pat on the back.

"I'll take you to them." Adair smiled as he led Halona to the archery area.

The Arian soldiers stopped what they were doing to bow to Adair as the duo approached. The Avory soldiers put their fists over their chests in respect to Halona.

"At ease," Adair said, before raising his hand. The archers set their bows down to listen to their prince. Halona responded to her people by placing her fist over her own chest.

Adair began to address the Arian archers. "This is Halona. She is the Avory Princess. She will oversee the archers in the upcoming war. You are to respect her. Disrespecting Princess Halona means disrespecting me."

Many of the men stared at the prince in shock. They could not believe that a savage woman was their superior. Many grumbles could be heard throughout the crowd, but there were no protests from the Avory archers.

"If anyone disrespects you, let me know." Adair looked at her seriously. "It won't be tolerated. We don't have time for our cultural differences to get in the way."

Halona nodded. She thought about changing the subject, but with so many of his men nearby, she needed to get him somewhere private. She gave an order to the archers to continuing practicing and making arrows. It took several minutes for everyone to listen. Adair had to send threatening glances toward several of the men.

Once the archers were busy, Halona turned to Adair. "How are you doing?"

"I'm fine," he lied.

"Adair," she crossed her arms with a sigh.

Adair shook his head. "If we don't focus on the war, we'll lose. We can't afford to have our minds filled with anything else."

Halona nodded and did not say anything else. Adair gave her a nod as he excused himself to go back to the soldiers. She watched his back as he walked away. She sighed and looked up at the blue sky. She saw the moon's shape in the distance and said a quiet prayer before turning to her subordinates.

The next morning was the day of departure. The army was as ready as it could be in so little time. The plan was for the army to advance toward the Orasi's territory. Information had been leaked to Elias that the Ivane were planning on attacking the Orasi where they bordered the three countries. If the Orasi lands were lost, it would allow the armies from Uron and the Ivane access to the center of Aria.

Halona and her archers were at the back of the precession while Adair and Liam were leading in the front with Roka and Callahan. Severin had command of the cavalry and Evian was a solider under Liam's command.

The army marched quickly. The goal was to make it to the Orasi before the Ivane. If Elias's calculations were right, they had four days. The army managed to make it a day early.

The evening of the third day, Roka and Adair's forces merged with the Orasi army. Callahan met up with his father as soon as they had reached the Orasi territory. The army continued marching to stop the Ivane and Uronian armies. Camp was set up a couple of miles from where the fighting would take place. The largest tent was used as a meeting place for the commanders to strategize.

Elias had a map stretched out on a large table. He pointed to the small area halfway between the Orasi and Ivane territories.

The area was on the exact border where the three countries met and where the battle was expected to take place.

"We can separate our armies to attack the Ivane from three different sides," Elias spoke. "My men will attack from the West."

Roka nodded, agreeing with the plan. "My men and I will attack from the South." He turned to Adair, "That leaves you to attack from the North."

Adair nodded. "Alright, but we'll have to plan it so the armies meet the Ivane at approximately the same time."

"He is correct. If we get the least bit overpowered by the Ivane, we could be defeated." Elias sighed.

"My men will head out in the middle of the night," Roka explained.

Adair nodded. "My troops will leave then as well. We can use the cover of night to get us into position without the enemy knowing.'

"Now that is settled…" Elias pointed to a small area off the North side of the battle field. "There are old ruins here. If we can get archers there, we will have a perfect shot at the enemy. Halona and her archers can move in from the north with Adair."

Roka nodded. "It's a good plan, but if we keep the archers in the same spot, the Ivane will eventually notice."

Halona glanced at the map before answering for Elias. "I can move them to a different spot when I get an opportunity. If we stay on the move, they won't know where the arrows will come from next."

Elias nodded. "That would work, but try to stay out of sight."

Halona nodded and glanced at Adair. He seemed to be deep in thought. Her father seemed to be thinking as well.

"There is a chance that the Ivane will be looking for the Peace Bringers," Roka's gruff voice spoke out. "You two will have to cover your destiny marks."

Adair nodded. "I was thinking the same thing, but I might have an idea." The other commanders in the room looked toward the young man as he continued. "You wear war paint, correct?"

When he received a round of nods, he continued, saying, "What if my men and I disguised ourselves as your warriors. They would not know that the Avory and Orasi were working with Aria."

Agreement echoed around the table. The meeting continued and then the commanders were sent out to their troops. The Ivane were expected to arrive the very next day.

Chapter 33

Hold still," Halona laughed as she painted Adair's face. The prince was squinting and squirming while she applied the green war paint to his face. The goal was to cover his destiny mark. She had already applied her red paint that signaled her as an archer. The two were sitting in a field as their troops readied themselves for battle.

"This stuff smells." He wrinkled his nose. "What is it made from?"

"If I told you, you would wash it off." Halona laughed.

"You're probably right," he said with a chuckle as she finished the last of her painting. She stepped back to examine her work and she smiled. Adair now had a green strip running from the middle of his forehead and down the center of his face. It covered the top of his nose and the center of his lips. She drew three horizontal lines on each cheek to symbolize his status as a commander.

"What does this paint design mean?" He traced his fingers along the red paint on her face. A semi-circle started on the center of her forehead and went counter-clockwise along her face. It stopped on her chin. A red streak connected the two points through the center of her face. She had the three commander lines as well as a small, red dot under each line.

"The semi-circle represents the bow and the dots represent that I am the child of a clan leader," she nodded. She leaned her face into his hand as he cupped her cheek.

"Be careful out there today," he said, looking down at her.

She gave him a small smile and nodded. "You be careful too."

He nodded. He stared down into her eyes as he let go of her cheek. He took her hand in his and slowly leaned his face down. A loud horn wailed through the area. Their eyes snapped in the direction of the pending battle.

"Duty calls," Halona said as she blushed.

"Yeah." Adair sighed and quickly kissed her on the forehead. "Be safe."

"You too," she whispered as the two separated to start the battle.

Halona led her archers to the top of the ruins. Adair followed her to the top to deliver a speech to his men. The painted faces of the men of Aria stared back at him.

Adair cleared his throat. "Today we make history! We will be fighting alongside our new allies against a common enemy. The Ivane and Uron want to conquer this world! I refuse to stand by and do nothing. Together with our allies we will bring peace back to Salacir!"

The Arian troops responded to their heir by raising their weapons in the air and letting out a large cheer. Halona and her archers responded as well with their own loud, war cry.

Before Adair stepped down from the ruins, he gave Halona one last glance as she was getting her archers into place. She flashed him a quick smile before he disappeared.

Halona had her archers in place and ready to fire as soon as the enemy came into sight. Once the front lines of the advancing army dropped, Adair and his men would charge.

"Get ready!" Halona called out as she held up her own bow. She watched as the enemy army began advancing. "Steady!"

The enemy reached closer. She waited for what seemed like an eternity before she gave the order.

"Fire!" She bellowed.

Suddenly, arrows began colliding with the advancing army. Men began dropping.

"Keep firing!" Halona shouted as she shot an arrow at the men below.

Severin's cavalry began charging. More men dropped dead as they swung their swords. Blood flowed along the battlefield making the dead grass turn red in the autumn morning.

Adair stood behind the archers with his footmen waiting for the second signal. When it came, they charged.

"Charge!" he shouted. The men began running toward the Ivane army. Adair ran as fast as he could past the ruins. He stabbed the first man he saw through the chest. The man's body crumpled to the ground after he removed his sword. He swung at another man and cringed when his sword buried itself in the man's neck. He sliced down through the man's chest as he removed his sword.

Halona watched from above as Arian troops fought the Ivane and Uronians below her. She saw Adair fighting a man when another came at the prince from behind. Before the man could strike, she embedded an arrow in the back of the would-be attacker's skull.

The man fell to the ground. Adair took care of the other man on his own. He hacked at the man's legs. The man dropped to the ground as Adair plunged his sword into the man's back. He pulled out the sword just in time to embed it into an Ivane woman.

A large shadow was cast over the troops before a loud crash was heard. Adair turned and saw part of the ruins were demolished. Bodies of the dead and injured littered the stone piles. The archers who were still alive continued to fire.

"They have catapults!" someone screamed from the battlefield just as a large boulder came crashing down onto several soldiers.

Another boulder hit the ruins. Halona had to think fast to keep her archers safe. She had lost a quarter of her unit between the two boulder strikes.

"Fall back!" she yelled to her troops. "If we stay here, we'll be crushed."

Adair watched from below as Halona and the rest of her archers ran from another boulder flying at them. He swung his sword to save another man from an attacker. The man gave Adair his thanks before they ran back into battle.

Adair tried not to think about Halona while he fought, but her safety began trailing in and out of his mind. He panted heavily as sweat began to collect on his skin. His thoughts became so cloudy that an enemy arrow managed to pierce his left arm. He cried out in pain and tried using his uninjured arm for fighting.

By the end of the day, the allied armies had been pushed back. They had begun to divide themselves to take care of the threats in the north and south. The armies heading west were getting closer to the heart of the Orasi territory. The Ivane had advanced far. The battle ended with the allied armies having to pull their camp back into the Orasi territory. The first day of fighting had ended. Adair and Halona had managed to bring their troops back to the safety of the Orasi's territory for the time being. More bloodshed would come.

Roka swore as he stared at the map. "We need to get rid of those catapults before they kill any more of us!"

Everyone else agreed, but strategies to take out the weapons were being bounced around.

"Could we build our own in time to counter theirs?" Callahan looked over at his father.

Elias shook his head. "No, we don't have enough time. Tomorrow we'll just have to hope that they don't advance any further. We lost many men, but we need to win this."

Chapter 34

Halona opened her eyes to see the bright blue color of the sky. Confused, she glanced around looking for the battlefield, but she could not find it. Instead, she was at the lake back in her home territory.

Suddenly, she heard a familiar voice ringing through the air, calling her name.

"Mother?" she shouted as she spun in a circle looking for the source of the sound of her mother's voice.

"Halona, come here my child." Elexia's voice echoed through the area.

"Mother!" she screamed as she began running toward the sound.

Halona ran as fast as her short legs could carry her. She ran until she reached the small area within the trees where her mother was buried. She paused when she saw her mother standing above the grave.

"Mother," Halona spoke softly.

Elexia gave her daughter a warm smile as she opened her arms. Halona sprinted to her mother and wrapped her arms around her mother's waist. Elexia placed her hand on her daughter's head. Her fingers ran through Halona's red hair.

"Halona, I came to warn you." Elexia looked down at her daughter's face as she spoke.

"Warn me?" Halona stared up at her mother.

Elexia nodded and began speaking. At first, her words were coherent, but they soon turned into gibberish.

Halona watched as her mother's bright, green eyes turned black.

"Mother?" Halona took a step back. Elexia's eyes were now completely black. Her red hair turned grey. Blood began to drip from her lips. Her mouth opened and she let out an ear-piercing scream.

Halona covered her ears and took another step away from her mother. Elexia's mouth twisted into a wicked grin.

"What's the matter, Halona?" A voice spoke that was clearly not Elexia's voice. This voice was deep and dark while Elexia's voice was warm and comforting.

Halona shook her head to get herself out of her nightmare. She turned and bolted from the area. She made it through the arch just before it collapsed. The sky darkened around her as the trees began to die.

Halona panted as she leaned against a tree to catch her breath.

"What was that?" She spoke to herself. Her eyes widened as the creature her mother had turned into walked right through the debris.

"Come here, Dear. Come see your mother." The dark voice cackled. Elexia's nails and teeth had grown long and pointed.

"You aren't my mother!" Halona shrieked as she turned to run away. She ran through the woods until she made it to the lake. Standing at the edge of the water was Mariana.

"Mariana!" Halona cried out for help.

Mariana's head made a complete turn to look at Halona. The young girl stopped in her tracks and stared in fright.

"Mariana?" Halona whimpered.

"Halona," The same dark voice from before came from Mariana's mouth.

Halona froze in fear as she heard the leaves crunching behind her. She glanced quickly and saw the fake Elexia walking toward her.

Halona ran once again from the two figures, now finding it hard to outrun them. They were right on her heels.

"Leave me alone!" she shouted. In her frantic escape, she was not paying attention to where she was going. She tripped over a large tree root and hit the ground.

She screamed and shut her eyes as the figures grew closer and closer.

"Leave me alone!" she shouted once more. They were getting closer. She had nowhere to go.

She felt a warm presence and a bright flash of light caused her to open her eyes. A woman stood over her with hair the color of the night sky and skin was as pale as snow. A glow as bright as the stars surrounded the woman's body.

"Mistress Moon." The words came off Halona's lips in a whisper.

The woman turned to give Halona a smile. "Hello, Halona."

Halona scrambled to her feet to bow to the woman. She put her hand over her heart.

"Rise, child." The woman's melodic voice echoed through the area.

Halona found herself rising without a second thought. She looked past the woman and saw two black piles of goo.

"Is that what I think it is?" Halona pointed to the piles.

The Moon Spirit nodded, "Those are the demons that were chasing you. They took the form of your loved ones to try and take over your mind. You must be careful."

Halona gave a quick nod. "But be careful of what?"

"When you dream, these demons will take your spirit and happiness. You must not give into the fear, for that makes them stronger," the spirit explained. "They thrive on guilt and fear."

"Guilt and fear," Halona whispered.

Mistress Moon nodded. "You are still feeling guilty for your mother's and Mariana's deaths."

"But…" Halona began to speak.

The Moon Spirit cut her off. "You may deny it, but it does not change the truth. You must rid yourself of the guilt you feel from their deaths and the fear of losing anyone else."

"How do I do that?" Halona looked to the woman for answers, but the woman only shook her head.

"I'm sorry, Halona, but that is something you must learn on your own." Once she finished speaking, she disappeared.

Halona's eyes fluttered open, revealing that she was in her tent. She was not alone. She turned her head to see Adair awake and looking down at her, his arms wrapped around her waist.

"Good morning," he said with a smile.

Halona frowned in confusion, "When did you get here?"

Adair shrugged and let her go as he sat up. "I was making rounds and checking on my injured men when I heard you whimpering as I passed your tent. I thought something was wrong, but you were only having another nightmare. I decided to stay with you until morning."

She nodded. "We attack at noon. Right?"

He smiled. "Yes, the sun is just starting to rise. If you weren't up soon, I was going to wake you."

Halona shook her head as she stood. "No, I'm fine. We should make sure our soldiers are awake."

He pulled his tunic and armor back on. Halona turned her face to hide her blush and to keep herself from staring at his bare chest. She sat up and began pulling her armor on as well. "Are we painting faces again?"

He shook his head. "No, it did not do anything but waste time preparing. It was an awful idea."

"I didn't think so," she said.

He rolled his eyes and smiled. "I exchanged letters with your father and Elias. My army will skip paint today to give the others an advantage. We're attacking first to catch them off guard."

The duo paused as an Avory messenger arrived. "Princess Halona," he said and handed her a letter. "Orders from your father."

She nodded as the messenger bowed to her before running off. Halona opened the letter. Adair peered at it from over her shoulder.

Halona,

We have determined that the catapults are technology from Uron. I want your archers to move to another location once the battle starts. There are hills to the east, not far from your current location. There is a perfect view of the battlefield and plenty of cover to keep the catapults away from you. Your job is to take out the Uronian soldiers working the catapults. Please respond after the battle with your progress. You should leave for the hills as soon as possible.

Good luck,
Roka

Halona looked to Adair, "Looks like I'm headed east as soon as I get everyone together."

Adair nodded. "Be careful."

She gave him a small smirk. "You know I will."

He let out a small chuckled and tucked a stray hair behind her ear. "I'm serious. I don't want to lose you."

"I will be fine, Adair," she whispered as she took a step toward him. She stood on her toes and slowly leaned in. Adair's musky scent filled her nostrils as she closed the gap between their lips by grabbing Adair and pulling him toward her. The stubble along his face tickled her cheeks.

Adair's hands wrapped themselves around her waist. Her lips were softer than any other woman he had shared a kiss with. She smelled sweet and tasted like honey.

The kiss seemed to last forever, and when Halona pulled her lips away from his, neither one of them could do anything but smile.

"Please be careful, Halona," Adair whispered in a soothing voice.

She brought her hand up to touch the whiskers on his chin. "Don't worry, Adair. We'll come back to each other safe." The calmness in her voice seemed to settle Adair's nerves.

He nodded and gave one of her hands a squeeze.

She stood forward on her toes to reach his lips. She placed a quick kiss on his mouth before she ran to her soldiers.

Adair stood in shock as he watched her disappear. She was finally his and he could not be happier. He looked up at the sky and smiled. "Now I know how you always felt around Alicia, my friend," he said, thinking of his friend Bennett.

◇•◇•◇

Chapter 35

Halona and her archers made it to their hill spot with a few hours to spare before the battle was to start. The hills her father had sent them to were more like small mountains. They had the perfect cover from the catapults, but men could easily ambush them on foot if she was not careful. They had to keep their position a secret.

"Make sure you stay quiet," she ordered. "We cannot alert the enemy to our presence."

She sat down to work on making more arrows. She took several sticks from a nearby tree and several rocks from the hard ground beneath her. She pulled out her knife to carve the sticks and rocks into the shape she needed. She watched as many of her archers were carving their own arrows as well.

The time to start the battle came quickly. She could see her father's army and Adair's army advancing to attack the enemy camp. She created two divisions for her archers. Half went to help shoot foot soldiers on the battlefield and the other half helped her shoot at the catapults.

"Our main targets are the men working the catapults, but if you can find a way to destroy the weapon, do it!" she shouted as she readied an arrow.

"Fire!" she shouted. Arrows showered down on the battlefield. Men and women began dropping. When someone behind a catapult was hit, another person replaced them.

Halona tried to have her warriors shoot as often as possible to keep anyone from firing the catapult, but they were not fast enough. Bodies were scattered as a large boulder hit the allied army. She called more archers over to help hit the catapults. They barraged the weapons with arrows. The people firing and loading the weapons dropped in masses, but were quickly replaced.

That's when an idea hit her. Remembering a lesson from Mariana, she thought of a way that she could quickly make a fire.

"Our magic is mostly used for healing," Mariana lectured. "But it can also be used to create fire or light."

"How?" Halona looked at her. She always wanted to make fire.

"Concentrate less on controlling the magic and focus on fire. Imagine a small ball of fire in your hand."

Halona did as she was told, but she was never able to make a ball of fire.

This time, Halona put all her focus into creating a ball of fire. She needed this to work. She tried and tried for several minutes before she saw the spark. The tiny flick of fire gave her more hope and determination. She kept at the magic until a small ball of fire floated in her hand.

"Light your arrows and aim for the catapults!" she shouted. She watched as her archers lit their arrows one-by-one, letting the arrows fall at the catapults. One caught fire instantly. The rest were surrounded by small fires lit by the arrows. Normal arrows were shot at the men trying to put out the flames.

"Again!" she shouted. She and her archers continued the process until all her fire was gone. Three of the seven catapults were on fire. The rest were surrounded by smaller fires. It slowed the catapult users down and allowed the armies advancing toward the enemy to gain more ground.

When Halona thought they had the upper hand, the enemy surprised them. She looked over the mountain's edge to see men pointing up at her archers.

"We've been spotted," she shouted as she shot several more arrows down at the men below.

She watched as a catapult was loaded. She ordered her soldiers to step back out of the way while she fired arrows.

"Ma'am, this is nuts!" one of her Avory archers said.

"I said get back!" she shouted at him. The man nodded and took a step back.

As Halona was loading another arrow, she and the rest of her archers felt the mountain shake. The boulder from the catapult had not made it to the top of the hill where Halona's archers were placed. Instead, it hit the side of the mountain and caused some of the cliff to crumble beneath them.

"Start firing again!" she ordered. She formed another ball of fire in her hands for another barrage of fire.

When the arrows hit, one more catapult blazed. Again, her archers shot fire into the enemy below.

"Shit." Halona cursed as she watched the catapult users light something on fire and throw it in her direction.

"Duck!" she screamed. She and her soldiers hit the deck as fast as they could. The fireball coming near them came higher than the boulders before. The ball of fire flew over their heads and rolled down the small mountain. It lit everything it passed on fire.

"Shit," Halona swore once more.

Her archers looked to her for an order.

She turned toward the battlefield below and frowned when she noticed a small army moving toward the mountain.

"Take out that army," she commanded.

She received salutes as arrows began firing down at the advancing army. Another boulder crashed into the mountainside followed by another fireball. This fireball was lower than the others and took out a group of her archers.

Halona tried not to panic. She found herself looking to the sky for answers.

"Please, help us, Mistress Moon," she whispered before firing arrows back down at the enemy.

The army coming toward them was losing men, but not fast enough. They were coming quick and Halona needed to think fast. Her remaining archers continued to shoot arrows at the army and at the catapults.

Frowning, she thought of an idea. She wasn't sure that it would work, but it was worth a shot. She tore a piece of cloth from her sleeve and cut her finger to write on it with her blood. She wrote a quick message for help. She tied the cloth around an arrow. She ran to the side of the mountain where she could have a good shot to someone. She fired it and prayed that it found its way to someone who could help.

She returned to firing arrows at the army below. They were getting closer. Things were looking bad.

dair panted as he pulled his blade from the body of an enemy. An arrow whizzed past his head and landed in the dirt. He looked toward Halona's archers. Why would they fire in his direction?

He saw the enemy army advancing up the mountain toward the archers.

"Damn it," he swore as he shoved his sword into another man. He wanted to help, but he was not able to do anything.

alona cursed as she shot another arrow. They were going to be attacked and she could not prevent it.

She sighed and watched as an arrow embedded in a man's forehead. She aimed again and shot another man in the leg.

"How are we doing on arrows?" she asked, turning toward another archer.

"We are running low, Princess," he said as he looked at her solemnly.

Halona took in a deep breath and nodded, "Tell everyone to start firing at the catapults. If we can take the rest out, maybe we can turn the tide of battle for the soldiers on the battlefield."

"But what about us?" He looked at her. He already knew the answer. They would be killed or captured.

"We can only hope for the best. Now, start shooting at those catapults," she ordered. The man nodded and rushed off to tell the others. Halona barked her order once more and soon she was the only one defending the archers. The others shot at the catapults and managed to destroy one more. There were two left.

Halona continued to shoot at the army. From the corner of her eye she saw the last two catapults catch fire. Her archers began shooting at the advancing army once again. Several soldiers dropped.

The army was getting too close. Halona and her archers were trapped between the fire behind them and the soldiers ahead of them.

"Keep shooting!" she ordered. She dropped a man to his knees with her arrow. Several more followed until very few soldiers were left to fight. By the time they reached the top of the mountain, only a quarter of the army was left.

The army shouted as they charged toward the archers. Halona brought out a knife from her boot. She stabbed it into a man's neck. Blood spurted from his wound and covered her as he dropped to the ground. Around her, other archers either fired arrows or used knives to defend themselves.

Halona hit another man in the ribs with her blade. She twisted the knife before pulling it out. The man grabbed his wound and howled in pain. He managed to stab Halona in the shoulder before he collapsed to the ground. Halona hissed in pain. She took her knife and slit the man's throat.

"Bastard," she muttered. Another man charged at her. Her knife found its way to the man's forehead. He slumped to the ground. She panted as she gripped her injured shoulder. She would not be able to use the arm until it healed. The wound was not deep, but blood continued to slowly soak her shirt.

Bodies covered the hill. She and her archers fought for an hour to defend themselves from the attack. It was not until the last enemy dropped that they could relax.

The battle below was almost over. The Ivane and Uronian armies had been pushed back. Halona was doing her rounds and looking at the bodies. She was counting which bodies were her archers and which were enemies. A hand with a large knife stretched up from the body of an attacker. The blade embedded itself deep into her thigh, causing her to scream in pain and fall to the ground. One of the other archers heard her and rushed to her aid to subdue the enemy.

"Princess," someone shouted as they rushed to her side. The knife was deep in her thigh and blood poured from the wound. Halona tried to wave them off. She grabbed the closest person to her in an attempt to stand and steady herself as her vision began to fade.

Chapter 36

dair searched the camp for Halona. The armies had merged back together once they gained territory. The Ivane were trapped between the army, the Etrasian Mountains, and a large river. They would be slaughtered, drown, or get lost in the untamed mountains.

Something felt off as he walked passed the tents. He noticed many of Halona's archers sitting along the aisle between tents. Some were bandaged while others bandaged their comrades. Adair stopped at a couple holding one another as they bandaged their wounds.

"Where's Princess Halona?" Adair asked.

The two of them pointed to the medical tent down the path.

"She was injured when we were attacked," the man spoke softly.

Adair never gave the man and woman his thanks. He was too worried to think of anything but Halona. He silently prayed to any deity that would listen that she would be okay.

His pace quickened when an ear-piercing shriek echoed through camp. Standing outside of the tent were Severin and Evian. They looked up at Adair as he approached.

"She's fine," Severin spoke before Adair could ask about Halona's condition. "She's being healed by Lilith right now."

Another scream ripped through the air causing the two brothers to flinch. Adair pushed past them as he flung the flap of the tent open.

Roka, Lilith, and another Orasi healer were standing over a cot with Halona on it. Sweat was dripping from her face and a blanket was her only form of cover. One healer worked on her shoulder while Lilith worked on her thigh. The pain from her healing skin caused her to scream again. Roka stood beside his daughter with his hand in hers.

"Halona." Adair's worried tone caused her head to snap in his direction. She cursed as he rushed to her side. He stood beside Roka to stay out of the way of the healers.

"Hey," she muttered weakly. Sweat caused her hair to stick to her face, so Adair pushed it out of her eyes.

"What happened?" he asked, glancing over her injured body.

She opened her mouth to speak, but another wave of pain rippled through her body. He slipped his hand into her hair to comfort her. She managed to give him a weak smile before slipping into unconsciousness from the pain.

Adair turned to Roka. "What happened to her?"

"A small army made it up the hill. She had to use hand-to-hand combat to defend herself and her archers. One stabbed her in the shoulder. Another stabbed her in the thigh after the battle when she was looking over the dead."

"I saw she needed help," Adair hissed and clenched his fist. "I should have helped her."

"Don't be stupid," Roka scoffed. "There was nothing you could have done and you know that. She's alive. That's what is important."

Adair turned to look at the man dumbfounded. He could have saved Halona. Hell, either one of them could have helped her. Why was he being so nonchalant about it?

Adair was about to open his mouth to criticize the Avory leader, but he saw the worry in the man's eyes. Roka was terrified. He could see the guilt in the man's eyes. He had given Halona the order to take her archers to that large hill.

"It isn't your fault either," Adair muttered. "We couldn't have kept her out of battle even if we wanted too."

Roka let out a deep chuckle. "You have a point. The girl is stubborn."

Adair nodded. "I've noticed."

"Tell me something, Adair." Roka glanced at the Arian Prince. Adair gave the man a glance back.

"Do you love my daughter?"

Adair flinched. He had not expected that to be Roka's question. Did he love Halona?

"I don't know," Adair answered honestly. "I care for her. I care about her a lot, but I wouldn't say my feelings are love."

Adair tensed as he waited for the man's answer. Roka only nodded.

"I do think I could eventually love her. I know I want her in my life and that I wouldn't know what to do with myself if she were no longer in it," Adair continued.

Roka nodded once more and released his daughter's hand. "Do me a favor then," Roka said. He turned to stare down at Adair. "Promise me you will protect her."

Adair gave the man a serious stare and nodded. "With my life."

Roka clasped Adair's shoulder. He gave the young man a nod as he walked from the tent unable to watch his daughter any longer.

Adair pulled up a chair beside Halona's cot as he watched her sleep. He ran his fingers through her hair and placed a soft kiss to her forehead.

The flap to the tent opened once more and Liam stepped in. He was panting and sweaty from sprinting to the medical tent as soon as he heard the news that his sister was injured.

"How is she?" he stuttered, out of breath.

"Healing," Adair said.

The Avory heir nodded and pulled up his own chair. "Father thinks our final battle will be tomorrow. We have the Ivane down in numbers and they are trapped. It's only a matter of time before they surrender or we slaughter them."

Adair nodded and leaned back in his chair. He stared at Halona's sleeping form before a question came to him.

"Liam, do you want to lead your people?"

Liam seemed taken aback by the question. It was unexpected. He let out a sigh and shook his head. "I'm the oldest of my father's children. It's my destiny. It's my duty."

"Couldn't you pass the leadership on to one of your brothers?"

Liam nodded. "I've thought about it. Severin would make a much better leader than me."

Liam's face took a solemn look as he stared down at Halona.

Adair nodded again. "You're lucky that you have so many siblings."

Liam chuckled. "It was never boring growing up."

Adair chuckled. "Like I said, you're lucky."

Liam laughed along with him. They both turned toward the girl on the cot when they heard her groan. Halona's eyes slowly opened and she stared up at them.

"Is it over?" she mumbled.

Adair laughed softly as he nodded. "They couldn't finish healing you with their magic. They have to let you heal on your own."

Halona frowned and sat up, hissing in pain, "Damn it."

"Careful, Sis," Liam frowned.

"I'm fine," she grumbled as she tried to swing her legs over the side of the cot. She groaned again and fell forward. Adair gently caught her and helped her lay back down.

"You need to stay there," both men lectured, earning a frown from her.

"Shut up," she snapped bitterly.

Adair began to chuckle which caused her to look at him confused. He kept laughing.

"What is wrong with you?" She raised an eyebrow.

"This seems familiar," he chuckled. "Only you're the injured one."

Halona's eyes rolled, but she found herself laughing along with him despite the pain in her body.

Liam gave her head a few pats before he stood. "I'll leave you two lovebirds alone."

Their laughing stopped and was replaced with silence. Liam broke it by laughing as he stepped from the tent.

"You didn't keep your promise," Adair looked down at her with a serious look.

"Don't scold me," she frowned. "Just be romantic and kiss me while saying how happy you are that I'm alive."

Adair laughed and it was his turn to roll his eyes. "I'm happy you are alive," he leaned down to capture her lips in a quick and soft kiss. "Better?"

Halona's frown turned into a smile. "Much."

Adair chuckled and pecked her forehead, "You're so strange."

Halona let out a soft laugh. "You like it."

She leaned forward this time to catch his lips in a wet smooch. Adair laughed and smiled down at her.

"I could get used to this," he smiled.

Halona rolled her eyes. "Don't expect me to always be the injured one."

He laughed again and kissed her forehead once more. Adair stayed by her side for an hour before Roka entered the tent as the two were sharing a kiss.

Roka cleared his throat, walking toward the cot. He put a hand on Adair's shoulder and squeezed, startling the poor young man. When Adair turned around, Roka was staring at him intently.

"Your father sent us reinforcements," Roka said as he looked toward Adair. "If you are done here, I suggest you come with me."

Adair coughed and sat up straight. "Okay."

He stood and gave Halona one more kiss before following Roka from the tent.

"One of them has a message for you from your parents," Roka explained.

"About what?"

Roka shook his head. "I did not ask. It is not my business."

Adair nodded as Roka led him to the messenger. When the prince arrived, the man bowed. He seemed frantic.

"Hello," Adair said and sat in a chair across from the man.

The man bowed again before sitting down. "Your father and mother are requesting your presence on Aria's eastern borders."

Adair sat up and frowned. "Why? I'm sure the battles are going well. I heard men rejoicing on my way here."

"You're Highness, King Roland has fallen ill," the man spoke solemnly.

Adair's eyes widened. His father had been fine the last time he saw him.

"My father is ill?" Adair frowned.

The man nodded. "His doctors say he will not make it much longer. He wants to see you before he passes. You are also expected to be crowned king after his passing. You will end this war as the King of Aria."

Adair froze. He knew he would be king eventually, but it was happening too soon.

He stood and nodded to the man. "I will take an escort with me. We will leave in an hour."

The messenger nodded before rushing off to find men to escort the future king.

Adair's breathing picked up. He rushed past Roka and headed back to the medical tent. He flew through the tent flap and looked at Halona.

Her eyes widened when she saw him. "Adair, you're crying!"

He had not realized it, but he was crying. He flopped into one of the chairs by her side and buried his face into the cot.

She ran her fingers through his long, brown hair while she watched him sob.

"My father is dying," he spoke between gasps. He was losing it.

"Adair," she said and stroked his hair. "I'm sorry."

He lifted his head and looked at her. His eyes were red and puffy. His face was streaked with tears. "I'm leaving for Aria's eastern border in an hour."

She nodded and did not say anything as she brought one of his hands to her lips.

"I'm going to be crowned King," he sighed and buried his face in her hair. He took in the sweet smell.

She gave him a small smile. "You'll be a great king."

He leaned up from her hair and sighed again, "It may be months before I see you again. It could even be years. It all depends on how much longer this war lasts."

Halona gave him another smile. "I'll wait. I can't do much in this condition anyway. You won't have to worry so much about me getting injured again."

He managed a small smile. "That's one good thing."

Halona placed her hand on the side of his face. "Go, Adair. Go see your father. Lead your people. Be the king they need."

He gave her a quick nod before grazing his lips against her soft ones. His fingers tangled in her hair and he continued to kiss her. She reached her good arm up to rest her hand on his chest. The two kissed for as long as they could to make up for the time they would lose.

Chapter 37

Halona remained in the medical tent healing while the latest battles took place. The Avory and their allies were winning. She was miles from the battlefield, but she could hear the distant sounds of the battle. An occasional battle cry would echo through the area.

She groaned and stared at the flap of the tent. Adair had been gone for days. She missed him, of course, but nothing would quell the boredom she was feeling. She half expected him to throw himself through the tent flap and kiss her once more. Her hands were itching to shoot an arrow, but everyone knew she was in no condition to go fight.

Lilith and a few of the other Orasi healers stayed behind in the tent to care for the injured.

"He'll be back," Lilith glanced over at Halona. She was healing one of Halona's archers that had been injured in the attack on the hill.

"I know," she frowned. "That's not what I'm worried about."

"You can't go out and fight either," Lilith scolded. "You can't even walk."

Halona continued to frown. Since when did Lilith care about her wellbeing?

"I'm a Peace Bringer," Halona grumbled. "I'm meant to end this war."

"You can't do anything right now, Halona," Lilith rolled her eyes. Halona's stubbornness was getting on her nerves.

"Watch me," Halona groaned as she slowly sat up. She hissed in pain and fell back onto the cot.

"I told you," Lilith smirked.

"Then heal me faster so I can go out there!" the redhead snapped.

Lilith raised an eyebrow. "You should know that a healer can only do so much. I don't have the skills that Mariana had. If you want healed, try it yourself."

Halona's eyes widened. Of course! Why had she not thought of that? She waved her hand and Lilith brought her a vile of paste from a shelf before she went back to working on the other injured soldiers.

Halona started with her thigh. If she could heal it, she could walk. She slowly unwrapped the bandages and grimaced. The cut was deep. She would have her work cut out for her. She took in a deep breath before she rubbed the paste into the wound. She hissed and sunk her teeth into her bottom lip. The burning never ceased.

Her vision blurred with tears as she focused magic into her palm. She let out a small whimper and bit her lip harder. Blood trickled down her chin.

"You can do this," she told herself. "You can do it."

The wound was healing, but not nearly as fast as she would have liked. She tried focusing more magic into the gash. The pain increased and she let out another pain-filled cry.

"Use the bond, Halona."

Halona blinked. Where had that voice come from? It sounded familiar, but she could not place who it belonged to.

"The bond."

Halona's eyebrow furrowed. What bond was this woman talking about?

"Adair."

Suddenly, it clicked. The bond between her and Adair. He had unknowingly used magic to help her months ago. If she could tap into that bond, she could heal her leg.

dair felt a warm presence inside as he and his escort raced to his father. They were on horseback, but it would still take them several days to return.

He paid no attention to the warm feeling in his belly. Instead, he focused on the ride.

alona panted as she stood. It had worked. Her leg was not healed completely, but it was healed well enough that she could walk. She bandaged the cut and smirked at Lilith.

"Look what I did," she gloated.

Lilith rolled her eyes. "How do you expect to use your bow when your shoulder is still injured?"

Halona's smirk fell. She had healed her leg, but healing her shoulder had not crossed her mind.

"Ugh!" she groaned and sat back down on the cot. Lilith chuckled and walked over to the girl.

"You are so stubborn," the Orasi woman shook her head. She unbandaged Halona's shoulder and started to rub the paste onto it.

Halona hissed and flinched as the pain returned. She placed her hand on Lilith's to help the girl heal the wound. Halona managed to tap into the bond between her an Adair once more. The wound closed enough that Halona would be able to use her bow, but it would be painful.

"Thanks," Halona said to Lilith.

Lilith nodded with a smile. "Go end this war."

Halona nodded and stood. She painted her face and pulled her furs and armor on. She picked up her bow and the quiver of arrows. She was going to do this.

She raced from the medical tent and mounted a horse as she raced for the battle field. She had one goal in mind.

She made it to the battlefield. Aria's forces were no longer painted to look like savages. The Arian crest rested proudly on their uniforms and armor. They fought against the Uronian army that had been sent as reinforcements. She bypassed the fighting as she looked for her people and the Ivane. She rode her horse to a high cliff where her archers were placed. The warriors and Arians that she had fought alongside in the previous battles looked surprised at her return.

"I'm back, Bitches," she mumbled. She walked past her archers and climbed higher on the cliff until she had a perfect view to the back of the Ivane's forces.

There she found her target. Shal, the Ivane leader stood on a horse giving orders to his men from the safety of the back of his army. She scowled. The Ivane leaders were cowards who always hid behind their people. His gold colored face paint and crown of bones easily gave him away as the Ivane leader. He could easily retreat if the army began to lose. Halona had no intention of letting him escape.

She readied an arrow and fired it into one of the man's guards. She ducked and hid when the men looked in her direction. There was no way her archers would have had that kind of a shot. She readied another arrow and waited. The men were on guard as they kept their leader close. They took several steps toward more men to protect their leader. Halona fired another arrow and pierced another guard through the heart. He dropped and she hid once more.

Shal was beginning to panic. He brought more men around him to protect him. Halona picked them each off, one-by-one. She knew she would not be able to take them all out on her own. She turned her head to the side and saw a few of her Avory archers standing at the base of her cliff.

"We've come to help, Princess," he said. Their arrows were ready.

She nodded with a smile. "Take out the guards. Leave the Ivane leader to me."

Her archers nodded and fired their arrows. Three more of Shal's guards dropped and Halona and her archers continued to fire until only a handful of the guards were left. She aimed an arrow at the leader and released it, watching it fly. It grazed his cheek only causing a large cut to stretch across it.

"Damn it," she hissed. Her shoulder screamed at her in pain, but she tried her best to ignore it.

Shal's remaining guards surrounded him until she could no longer see the leader. He had been pulled from his horse. The archers beside her never stopped firing arrows. More men dropped creating a perfect opening for her.

Halona took in a deep breath as she pulled her last arrow from her quiver. Her shoulder was still protesting as she knocked the arrow and pulled the bow string back. She fired the arrow and watched as it embedded into Shal's skull.

Chapter 38

dair arrived at his father's camp early in the morning. The sun had yet to peak over the horizon of hills that separated the Arian valleys from the desert of Uron. A man arrived to take him to his father's side. He followed the man to the tent where his father lay in bed. When he arrived, a doctor stood over his father. He looked up to see Adair standing in the doorway of the tent. He cleared his throat and bowed.

"Your Highness, I am afraid you are too late. Your father passed early this morning in his sleep."

Adair nodded and swallowed the lump growing in his throat. "Leave us."

The doctor nodded before exiting the tent with the man who brought the prince.

Adair sat on the stool next to his father's bed and cupped his hands together. "I am sorry, Father. I wish I could have said goodbye."

Tears dripped from his eyes, landing on his hands. He sat with his father in silence for several moments, letting the tears fall from his eyes until there were no more left. He stood and bowed to his father before reaching out to grasp the dead man's hand and squeeze it.

"You were a great king," he said. "And an even greater father."

He cleared his throat and wiped the remaining tears from his eyes. When he left the tent, an advisor, a bald man, was waiting for him.

"I am sorry for your loss, Your Highness," the advisor said. "Your father was a great man."

Adair nodded. "Thank you, but I believe we have business to attend too."

The advisor dipped his head before leading Adair to the tent where the battle plans were being made. He entered and was greeted by several more advisors. All of them gave him their condolences before getting down to business.

"With King Roland's passing, you are now king. There is no time for a coronation, but those plans can be made once we have won this war," the bald advisor said.

Adair stared at the maps below him with a hard gaze. The maps clearly outlined the eastern border of Aria. The enemy lines were marked in red ink and the Arian forces were marked in blue.

"Your Highness, perhaps you should stay behind and give orders from a safe distance?" the bald advisor said.

Adair shook his head. "No, I want to fight alongside my men."

"But Your Majesty," another advisor protested. "King Roland has just passed. We cannot lose Aria's current king before he has a chance to marry and produce an heir."

"I understand your concern, but I will fight alongside my men."

"Of course, Your Majesty."

Adair nodded. "Very well, have my horse prepared. We will end this war once and for all."

"Yes, Your Majesty."

"And see to it that my father's body is sent home so that my mother may bury him properly," Adair said before leaving for his horse.

Adair's horse was brought and he mounted it. Sitting tall on the steed, he looked out at the battlefield below. Bodies littered the ground from a battle days before he arrived. He took a deep breath, thinking of Halona laying in the medical tent at the northern camp. He took a deep breath before he sent his men charging toward the Uronian armies early in the morning. The plan was to ambush the resting army before the sun rose.

He took in a deep breath as he and his men began marching toward the enemy camp. This was not a normal Arian fighting style, but Adair could not lose this battle by using chivalrous tactics.

The Uronians were caught off guard by the approaching threat. They had not been warned in enough time. The Arian army marched in and began slaughtering the enemy. Adair searched for King Hedras.

The Uronian King was unprepared. When Adair found him, the man looked sloppy.

"King Roland sent his son in to attack," the King laughed as he unsheathed his sword. Adair dismounted his horse and unsheathed his own sword.

"My father has passed away," Adair seethed. "He fell ill. I am now King of Aria."

King Hedras scowled as he brought his sword up to point it at Adair. "Your father always was a pitiful man."

Adair's eyes narrowed as he swung his sword. He let out a loud cry as he swung. King Hedras blocked Adair's blow. The two continued to fight for several minutes. King Hedras dismissed his guards to fight with the rest of the army. He wanted to be the one to beat the new Arian King.

Around them, the Uronian soldiers dropped dead. Adair's sneak attack was becoming a success.

"If you surrender now," Adair offered. "I will spare your life."

King Hedras laughed. "I would never surrender to a brat like you."

The older man stabbed his sword toward Adair. The blade caught Adair's arm and tore through the sleeve of his shirt. He smirked as he saw a weak spot on the King of Uron. Adair pushed his sword into the opening and in one swoop, sliced off the older man's hand. King Hedras's sword dropped to the ground with a clank.

The King let out a loud and painfilled bellow. Adair took the opportunity to swipe his sword at the man's legs. The King dropped to the ground. Adair held his sword at the man's throat.

"You still have a chance to live Hedras." Adair towered over the injured man.

Hedras let out a guttural growl as he snatched his weapon from the ground with his only hand. Adair was quick to catch the man's attack, but not fast enough to block it. Soon, they were both impaled with a sword. Adair watched as the king's eyes rolled back and his body slumped further to the ground. His hand released the sword within Adair. Adair looked down at the blades between them. His sword had been buried deep into the older man's chest to the point where his heart was stuck on the end of the blade as it protruded from Hedras's back.

The sword that had pierced Adair was embedded in his shoulder. He stood as he heard voices coming toward him. He carefully turned his head to see men from his army running toward him.

"Your Highness!" They shouted as they rushed to their king's aid.

Adair smiled as he panted while the men ran to him. His vision was beginning to blur. It did not take long for his vision to fade to black.

dair's eyes fluttered open.

"Mother?" He groaned as he sat up.

Queen Abry put her hands on her son's chest to usher him back down into bed.

"You need to rest, Adair," she lectured.

"But the war," he groaned.

"The war is over," she said with a smile. "King Hedras is dead and his sons surrendered while you were unconscious."

"Who took the surrender?"

Queen Abry laughed. "I did. You didn't think your mother was a useless queen, did you? I controlled the armies while your father was ill. I took control again while you were unconscious."

Adair smiled. "You are amazing, Mother."

"I'm your mother." Queen Abry smiled. "Of course, I am amazing."

Adair laughed and smiled as he chatted with his mother. They could finally mourn the loss of King Roland as mother and son. They talked and cried as they discussed the man's life.

Hours later, a knock ended the conversation.

"Your Majesty," a guard said as he entered the room. "You have a letter from our Avory allies."

Adair's mother helped him sit up and rest against the headboard as the guard brought the letter to his king.

Adair unrolled the scroll.

To the King of Aria,

I'm writing to inform you that your allies, the Avory and Orasi, have defeated the Ivane and Uronian armies in the north. Aria's northern borders are safe from attack. I wish to invite you and your family to my village for a feast. You will be warmly welcomed as our friends. I wish you luck with the war on your eastern border.

Sincerely,

Roka of the Avory

Adair smiled and relayed the message to his mother. Her face turned pale at the thought of visiting a savage village.

"Maybe you should invite the savage leader and his family here," she suggested. "We can have a feast when the country finishes mourning for your father."

Adair nodded and reached to the nightstand for a quill and parchment. His mother smiled and handed it to him. He wrote to Roka. His mother rushed out to find someone to send the letter to the Avory leader. When she returned, she settled at her son's bedside once again.

"It's settled," Adair said with a sigh. "In two months, we will hold a feast to celebrate the end of the war. After our month of mourning is complete, I would like you to help me plan this, Mother."

Queen Abry smiled at her son and kissed his forehead. "I would be honored."

"And there is one more thing," Adair smiled slyly. He had one more thing that he needed to do.

Chapter 39

Halona stared in awe as she and her family entered the western gates of the Arian Capital. She could see the castle standing in the center of town. The massive stone structure towered over all the other buildings with several pikes that made the castle appear even taller. The last time she had been here, she had been met with animosity. This time, there were banners and decorations. Musicians played in the streets while dancers swung their bodies to the music. The city was alive with excitement and all of it was because her family was here.

"Are you ready to see your prince?" Liam teased his younger sister. Halona frowned and elbowed him in the side.

"He is king now," she growled. She could not hide her nervousness. Adair was king. It had been months since she last saw him. Would he still have the same feelings he had the last time they had spoken?

Evian wrapped an arm around his sister's shoulders. "Don't look so nervous. You may scare him off."

It was Evian's turn to get an elbow to the side. Guards met the group of Avory and Orasi to lead them to the palace safely. Many people were happy for their new allies, but old feelings still lingered.

"Excuse me, sir," a guard said, turning to Roka.

"Yes?" The Avory leader looked at him. The guard flinched under Roka's intimidating gaze and size.

"We were instructed to take you straight to King Adair." The man bowed. "He has an urgent matter to discuss with you."

"About?" Roka raised an eyebrow.

The guard shook his head. "He never said, Sir. I was only told to bring you straight to his majesty."

◇•◇•◇

Odair waited patiently in his chambers His guests had arrived. It was only a matter of time before Roka would be brought to him. He took in a deep breath. He was nervous. He twirled the small black box in his pocket.

A knock brought the king from his thoughts.

He cleared his throat before speaking. "Enter."

The door opened and a guard stepped in with Roka.

The guard bowed before Adair dismissed him. The young man rushed from his king's office and headed back to his post.

Adair offered Roka a seat, but the man preferred to stand.

"May I ask what this is about?" Roka raised an eyebrow.

Adair inwardly chuckled as he pulled the little black box from his pocket. He crossed the room to place the box in Roka's hand.

The Avory leader stared at it for a moment before opening it. Inside was a small, gold ring. One large diamond rested in the center while two smaller emeralds set beside it. Roka gave Adair a confused glance.

"I am not familiar with Arian customs," Roka said.

Adair mentally scolded himself for not realizing that this custom might be different for the Avory.

"I want to ask for your daughter's hand in marriage," Adair explained. His voice wavered, but he kept eye contact with Roka.

Roka closed the box and handed it back to Adair.

"In our clan, marriage proposals involve a weapon and the slaughtering of an animal," Roka spoke with a smirk. "Halona may be just as confused as I."

Adair cringed at the thought of Halona burying a knife into the throat of a lamb.

Roka and Adair arrived at the feast together. Everyone rose when the two entered. Halona's eyes met Adair's for a moment. He gave her a smile which she returned. Adair stood behind his seat and let his eyes travel over his guests.

His advisors stood on the left side of the table. His Avory and Orasi allies sat on the right. His mother sat directly beside him. He lifted his goblet and smiled.

"I would like to welcome the Avory to Aria's Capital and to my home," he began his speech. "Much has happened in the last several months, but I will cherish the allies Aria now has thanks to my time with the Avory. After the feast, my mother has prepared a party in the ballroom. Thank you again, and welcome to Aria."

He took his seat and the feast began. Musicians played in the corner while everyone ate. Adair's advisors seemed to be uncomfortable in the presence of their savage allies.

Halona took in Adair's features. His hair was trimmed and his dark whiskers were gone. He was clean cut and dressed in a grey suit.

Halona caught Queen Abry staring at her several times. Nervous under the woman's gaze, Halona kept her gaze on her plate as she ate.

Adair could have cut the tension with a knife. The feast was not going as smoothly as he had planned. He sighed to himself as he ate.

The feast ended in silence and everyone was ushered into the ballroom. More guests arrived as the music began to play. The dance floor soon filled with bodies as people began to dance. The savages remained on the outside of the party.

"This is so strange," Evian mumbled to his sister.

Halona glanced at him. "I know."

"Do you even know how to dance like that?" Liam came up behind her to tease. She frowned as her cheeks flushed.

Evian let out a loud laugh which caused many other guests to glance their way. "You'll be in trouble if Adair asks you to dance."

She brought her elbow up to jab her brother, but lowered it when their father cleared his throat behind them.

"Behave," Roka ordered.

"Yes, Father," the three mumbled. Halona's face paled when she noticed Adair across the room with another woman.

He had her hand in his and he placed a small kiss to the top of her hand.

"I'm going to throw up," Halona turned around. Tears threatened to spill from her eyes. She did not understand why she was so upset, but she wanted to leave.

"Calm down," Evian rubbed her back. "You're probably over reacting."

Liam smiled and bowed as Adair walked toward them with the girl on his arm.

"I would like you all to meet Lady Alya. Her family has been close with mine for decades." Adair smiled at the three siblings. Halona stared at the girl. Her curly blond hair and innocent, blue eyes seemed to mock her.

"Evian," Adair turned to the youngest brother. "Lady Alya is looking for a dance partner. I thought that I might be able to lead her to you."

Adair took the girl's hand and extended it toward Evian. Evian's eyes widened as he took the girl's hand.

"Uh," he said and stared between the two awkwardly. "Sure."

Lady Alya blushed and giggled softly as Evian led her to the dance floor.

Liam gave Halona a smirk and whispered, "I was right."

Halona rolled her eyes and elbowed her brother again, earning a laugh from Adair. He extended his hand to her.

"Would you like to dance?" He smiled at her.

Halona's cheeks flushed and she looked at the floor. "I don't know how."

Adair's laugh bounced off the walls. It was not a mocking laugh. It was more of a light tease. He took her hand in his and smiled at her.

"Just follow my lead," he whispered while he led her to the dance floor. Arian guests stared in awe at their king dancing with a savage woman. Whispers echoed throughout the ballroom.

"Are you alright?" Adair looked at her, worried.

"I'm fine," Halona said and turned her head away. She kept her eyes focused on their feet.

"Halona," he scolded. "I know you better than that."

Halona could not help but smile as she looked up at the young king. "This is all so strange. I'm used to feasts and parties being loud with lots of alcohol. I'm used to seeing people I know pass out drunk in the streets. All of this *properness* is intimidating."

Adair chuckled and leaned forward to press a kiss to her forehead. The whispers around them grew louder.

"People are staring at us like we're a spectacle." She blushed and looked down at her feet.

Adair winced when she stepped on his toes.

"Sorry!"

"It's just a foot," he teased. "And it is a spectacle. I am King of Aria, remember? Let everyone stare. They're just jealous."

"Of me?" She scoffed. "They're jealous of what your people consider an average savage girl?"

Adair chuckled softly. "You aren't average, nor are you a savage. I think you are wonderfully unique."

Halona rolled her eyes but kept smiling. "How are you doing?"

He let out a long sigh, "I'm doing alright. Seeing Bennett's wife was hard. She should be giving birth soon."

"How are you doing after losing your father?" She began to relax in his arms as she touched his cheek with her fingertips.

"I'm alright. It's been hard, but my mother and I have been supporting one another." He rested his head against hers.

"I've missed you," she said and smiled up at him.

"I've missed you too, Halona," he said as he tilted her chin up. His lips met hers. He groaned softly from the sweet taste. He had almost forgotten what kissing her felt like. When the two parted, everyone was staring. Halona caught Evian giving her a thumbs up from the side as he danced with Lady Alya.

Her cheeks flushed. "They're all staring at us."

Adair shrugged. "I can get them to stare longer."

"Fantastic." She laughed sarcastically as she shook her head. Adair put a hand over her eyes and laughed with her.

"Close your eyes. I have a surprise." He gave her nose a quick kiss.

Halona shut her eyes tight. She frowned when she felt Adair's hands leave her waist. She heard a collective gasp come from the crowd. Not able to contain her excitement any longer, she opened her eyes. What she saw confused her.

Adair was kneeling with a small black box in his hand. He smiled up at her and opened it. The ring inside the box did not do anything to help her confusion.

"Adair, what are you…" she began to ask, but Adair cut her off to explain.

"Halona, would you do me the honor of becoming my wife? I know this isn't how your people propose, but I want to spend the rest of my life with you and I am willing to kill a pig for you if that is what it takes. Hell, I would bathe in its carcass if it meant that you would be by my side for the rest of my life."

He took a deep breath as he waited for what seemed like an eternity for her answer. He watched as Halona stood there with her eyes wide. The room was silent as all waited for the girl to give the king an answer.

"Adair," she whispered as she reached out to touch the diamond ring in the box. The lights from the ballroom bounced off the large stone causing it to sparkle. Green dots flickered on her hand from the emeralds. She could not find words to leave her mouth. Instead of saying anything, she gave Adair a large smile and threw her arms around him. He lost his balance and laughed as he fell back onto his backside. She pressed her lips to his in a passionate kiss.

When she pulled back, he grinned at her and asked, "Is that a yes?"

She nodded and watched as he took her hand and slipped the gold band onto her finger. Tears dripped from her eyes as he kissed her once more.

Claps and cheers echoed through the ballroom as Adair rose to his feet with his future wife. He watched the faces of his guests. Some were clapping with large smiles. Others seemed put off by the idea of having a savage for a queen. His mother's reaction was the most important. Tears dripped from her eyes as she smiled at her son.

"I'm proud of you," she mouthed. "Congratulations."

Adair gave his mother a smile back before looking down at the woman in his arms. The large grin she gave him filled him with so much happiness that he could not help but kiss her once more.

Chapter 40

dair smiled to himself as he waited at the end of the aisle. Today was the day Halona would become his queen. The ballroom had been changed to make it the perfect setting for their wedding. He stared into the audience as he waited for his bride.

His mother sat at the very front. After today, she would no longer be Queen Abry. She would simply be the king's mother. In her lap, she was holding a small baby girl in her arms. Beside her sat the baby's mother, Alicia, with her small, baby boy on her lap. The twins already resembled their father and they were only a few months old. Lady Alya sat with her family and the rest of Adair's Arian advisors.

On the other side of the room sat Halona's family and clan. Her father would be walking her down the aisle. Her brothers sat in the front row trying to contain themselves. Evian kept winking at Lady Alya causing the young woman to blush. Lilith sat next to Severin with her hand in his. Their wedding would be coming within a few months.

Music began to play as the doors to the ballroom opened. All heads turned as people stood to await the future queen's arrival.

Adair's heart beat rapidly in his chest. This was it. He was marrying Halona. It seemed like only yesterday he had been in her care.

A large smile broke across his face when he saw her step through the large, wooden doors. Her father escorted her to the front. She wore a beautiful, lace gown as white as the snow falling outside the palace. The sleeves were long and the dress flowed past her feet. Her red hair was adorned with a crown of orange and purple flowers. More flowers were braided into her hair. She smiled when her green eyes met Adair's blue ones. Adair waited for what felt like an eternity as he watched Roka slowly lead Halona up the aisle to her future husband.

Roka placed Halona's hand in Adair's and kissed her forehead before he joined his sons in the front row.

"You look beautiful," Adair said as he smiled at her. Her cheeks flushed as she nodded. He could not help but chuckle.

The priest began to speak to the crowd behind the couple. "Today, two cultures will be brought together with the wedding of a lifetime. Our beloved King Adair will wed the Avory Princess, Halona."

Adair stared at Halona as he listened to the priest speak. Memories from the day they met until now played through his mind.

Halona stared at Adair also thinking of all the times they had shared. She had healed him when he was injured. She remembered the time they went to the lake outside of her village and the day they visited her mother's grave. She remembered how worried he had been when she was injured.

Adair took a few seconds to glance toward the back of the room. Standing against the wall were three people he did not expect to be there. Elexia and Mariana stood beside one another holding hands as they gushed over their beautiful bride. Bennett stood beside them. The look he gave Adair seemed to say, "I told you so."

Adair glanced at Halona and then back at the wall. The three were gone and it was time for the couple to exchange their vows and rings.

"You may now kiss the bride," the priest announced as he smiled at the couple.

Adair gave Halona a cocky grin as he pressed his lips to hers. He was delighted by the sweet honey taste and the smell of flowers that enveloped her. Her arms wrapped themselves around his neck. Their guests and people cheered as the king pulled his lips away from his queen.

Eyra took the place of the priest. In his hands, he held a crown. Halona took in a deep breath as Eyra began to speak.

"Do you promise to rule beside our king for the rest of your days?"

Halona nodded. "I do."

"Do you swear to serve Aria's people as our queen for all your life?"

She nodded once more. "I do."

"Should His Majesty be unable to fulfill his duties as king, do you swear to take over that role?"

Halona glanced at Adair before she nodded. "Yes."

Eyra nodded as Adair took the crown of flowers from her hair. He gave the flower crown to Eyra and took the silver crown. Adair smiled warmly at Halona as he looked down at her.

"Then I now crown you, Halona of the Avory, as Queen of Aria." Eyra announced.

Adair kissed her cheek as he placed the silver crown on her head.

"Ladies and gentlemen," Eyra shouted. "I now present you King and Queen of Aria!"

Halona smiled as her father replaced Eyra at the altar. He handed the newlywed couple a knife as he began to speak to the audience.

"As a symbol to the bond between our two peoples, the king and queen will perform an Avory marriage tradition."

The Avory guests shouted and cheered for the couple. Halona took the knife and sliced open her palm. Her father held up a bowl. She held her hand over it and watched as her blood dripped into it. She handed the knife to Adair who used it to slice open his own hand. His blood mixed with hers in the bowl.

Roka dipped his fingers into the couple's blood. He painted a full circle on each of their faces. Halona then dipped her fingers into the blood and painted a line through the center of Adair's face. Then she made a half moon on each of his cheeks. Adair dipped his fingers in and did the same thing to Halona's face.

They shared a kiss before turning toward their family and friends and clasped hands. While their hands were together, Halona used magic to heal the cuts. Roka handed Adair a rag to wipe the blood from their hands.

More cheers erupted through the crowd as the Avory swelled with pride. Adair reached down and picked his wife up. He kissed her once more as he carried her from the main ballroom.

Epilogue

dair paced back and forth in the hallway. He was nervous. He clasped his sweaty hands together. Had his father been this nervous?

He flinched when he heard Halona's screams coming from the room in front of him. He turned to Eyra and shook his head. Why was that man so calm?

"You look as nervous as your father did when you were born," Eyra gave the young king a pat on the shoulder. "Our queen will be just fine."

Adair shook his head. Halona's screams were growing louder by the second. He frowned and grabbed the handle of the door.

"Your Highness, you aren't allowed in there," Eyra spoke calmly.

"I am king. I will go wherever I damn well please. My wife is in there and I refuse to sit outside and twiddle my thumbs," Adair seethed as he threw open the door.

The women in the room stopped what they were doing to look to their king. Halona was in bed. Sweat coated her face and she was panting heavily.

"Your Majesty," one woman said as she looked toward him. "You shouldn't be in here."

"Let him stay," Halona said between pants. She gave her husband a painfilled smile. "After all, this is his child."

Adair gave his wife a smile and pulled a chair up next to her bed. He held her hand as she began to groan in pain. The other women in the room resumed their work and soon Halona's screams returned. Adair whispered calming words to her and gave her a forehead a soft kiss. Halona turned her head to scream obscenities at him before telling him to stay quiet and hold her hand.

Halona squeezed Adair's hand so hard it began turning purple. She panted and screamed while he continued to whisper soothing words in her ear.

Halona's screams were soon replaced by the cries of a baby. She leaned back, out of breath and smiling. Her head fell back against the pillow behind her as she watched the midwife clean the baby.

"That's our baby." She smiled at her husband and she played with his fingers. "That is our little one."

Adair smiled and gave her a loving kiss. He never got tired of the taste of honey. He pulled away in time to see his beautiful baby being swaddled and handed to his mother.

"Here you are, Queen Halona," the midwife said. She smiled as she placed the small bundle in the woman's arms.

"It's a boy," she said to the couple. "I'll leave you three alone to get acquainted. Don't hesitate to call if you need anything." She and the other women attending the birth quickly left the room.

Halona smiled at the swaddled baby in her arms. She ran her fingers through his dark hair. "He's beautiful."

Adair smiled and sat in the bed beside his wife. He pushed the blanket away from the baby's face. He grinned as he ran a dark finger along the baby's light brown cheek.

"He is," Adair could not hold in his excitement. "And he's ours."

Adair stood and opened the door to exchange words with Eyra. The man bowed and rushed off to fulfill his king's wish.

"What should we name him?" Adair asked as he crawled into the bed to be next to Halona and the baby.

"What about Bennett?" Halona looked up at her husband. Adair stared at her as his eyes became misty.

"Are you sure?" He blinked, surprised by the suggestion.

"He was an important part of your life." Halona smiled. "And we could always call him Bennie."

Adair chuckled and brushed a piece of hair from his wife's face. "It's perfect."

Halona smiled and brought the baby up to kiss his forehead. "Prince Bennett of Aria."

Adair smiled and stood when a knock sounded on the door. He crossed the room to open it. Two young, green-eyed girls came bouncing into the room. Their brown curls flopped on their heads as they ran.

"Papa!" They cheered as they pounced on Adair.

Halona chuckled and put a finger to her lips. "Girls, be quiet. Your brother is sleeping."

"Sorry, Mama," they whispered. Adair chuckled and brought his daughters into the bed with their mother so they could look at their baby brother.

"He's got hair like us and Papa," The smaller of the two spoke quietly.

"That's right Mari." Adair kissed the top of her head. "He does."

"What about his eyes?" The other asked as she leaned over her mother's side to get a better look at the baby.

"Sit back, Elexia. Give him space," Halona scolded. The little girl leaned back and looked up at her mother.

"What about his eyes, Mama?" she whispered softly.

"I don't know, Elexia. Be patient." Halona laughed as she kissed the top of her daughter's head.

"Will he be a king like Papa?" Elexia looked at her mother.

Halona and Adair shared a look with each other before looking down at their son. According to the current Arian Law, Bennett would be the next king. However, Elexia was the first born. They had discussed many times which of their children would rule the country in the future.

Mari giggled as Adair ran his fingers through her brown hair. "Braid it, Papa!"

Adair smiled and with a laugh started to sloppily braid her soft locks. She giggled quietly and watched her baby brother.

"What's his name?" Elexia leaned forward to kiss her brother's head.

"Bennett," Halona whispered as she kissed her Elexia's cheek. "His name is Bennett."

"Bananet," the girls tried to say the name. Adair laughed softly at their failed attempt.

The baby in Halona's arms began to cry. She bounced him in her arms. He stopped his crying as his eyes slowly opened.

"Blue!" Elexia shouted. Her shout caused the baby to cry once more.

"Alright, girls," Adair groaned. He stood and scooped his daughters up in his arms. "It's time to go."

Elexia and Mari whined and protested while Adair carried them from the room. Halona calmed the baby down once again and began to feed him.

Adair reentered the room and sighed. "Those two are a handful."

He collapsed into the bed beside his wife and began to run his fingers through her messy hair.

"Just like their father," Halona teased. Adair rolled his eyes and ran his fingers through the baby's hair.

"I would say you're more of a handful than I am. I distinctly remember you throwing a vase at one of my advisors," he frowned playfully as he poked her cheek.

"Hey!" She frowned. "He insulted my ability to be queen based on my heritage and gender. Besides, he shouldn't have upset me while I was pregnant."

Adair smiled and nodded, "You're even feistier than normal with a baby on the way."

"But you love me," she stuck her tongue out.

Adair laughed and captured his wife's lips in a kiss. "I do. I love you and the girls and this little boy."

Adair kissed the baby's head one more time. The small creature finished eating and Halona handed him to his father.

"There you are, sweetie," she smiled at both as she placed the baby in her husband's arms. Adair cradled the baby close to his chest. He slowly bounced him in his arms. Adair looked down at his third child. "My son," he whispered. He glanced at Halona and kissed her cheek. "My wife."

He had his family and his people. There was nothing that could make him happier. With Halona ruling by his side, the country was destined for greatness.

Acknowledgments

Three years of hard work went into *What Lies Beyond* and it is surreal to see it finally in print. I would like to thank those who helped and supported me along the journey. I would first like to thank the family for supporting me through this process.

I would like to thank the friends who attended Independence Community College with me. Thank you, Jordan Rausch, Annie Morton, Braidon Beard, and Jerusha Luker for the late nights of writing and support as I attempted to complete the first draft of *What Lies Beyond* in thirty days during National Novel Writing Month.

Thank you, Brenda Hogsett-Sanchez for sponsoring ICC's Creative Writing Club during my time there. Through your support, as well as many others from the club, I was able to complete the first draft of *What Lies Beyond*. I would also like to thank you for the thoughtful review.

I would like to thank Zachary Palmer for not only helping me edit my manuscript, but also for the thoughtful review. Thank you for allowing your home as a space for me to write and edit, and thank you for being an amazing Dungeon Master.

I would like to thank Ralvell Rogers II for his help in marketing *What Lies Beyond*, as well as all the work he put into helping this book become published.

I would like to extend a big thank you to Tracy Million Simmons and everyone else with Meadowlark for all their work with the cover, the editing, and formatting to help this dream become a reality.

Hannah Jeffers-Huser

About the Author

annah Jeffers-Huser was raised in Fredonia, Kansas. At the age of three she was diagnosed with leukemia. She has been cancer free for close to seventeen years and off of treatment for sixteen. She attended Independence Community College where she received her Associate of Science degree in secondary education. She is currently enrolled at Emporia State University and studying to be a middle and high school Social Studies teacher. She loves to travel, visiting places like London and Costa Rica. She is involved in Quivira, ESU's creative writing club, and plays Dungeons and Dragons regularly.

WWW.MEADOWLARK-BOOKS.COM

Specializing in Books by Authors from the Heartland since 2014

A MEADOWLARK BOOK

GREEN BIKE

a group novel by
Kevin Rabas, Mike Graves, & Tracy Million Simmons

Moon Stain
poetry by Ronda Miller

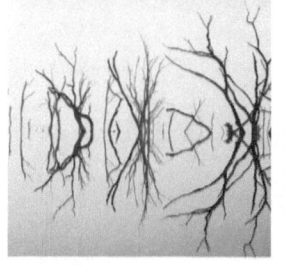
Water Signs
Poetry by
Ronda Miller

A Cow for College
and Other Stories of 1950s Farm Life

James Kenyon

A Life in Progress
and other short stories
Tracy Million Simmons

To Leave
a Shadow
Michael D. Graves

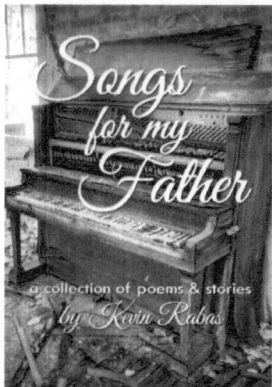
Songs
for my
Father
a collection of poems & stories
by Kevin Rabas

Walking on Water
poems
by
Cheryl
Unruh

Everyday Magic
Field Notes on the
Mundane and the Miraculous
Caryn Mirriam-Goldberg

Shadow
of Death
Michael D. Graves

Wandering Bone
Poems by
Olive L. Sullivan

www.ingramcontent.com/pod-product-compliance
Lightning Source LLC
Chambersburg PA
CBHW051248250626
47155CB00009B/3210